Xmas 2007

FOL 3

Susan,
Hope you … this book.
Linda

CORMAC
THE TALE OF A DOG GONE MISSING

BASED ON A TRUE STORY

SONNY BREWER

CORMAC
THE TALE OF A DOG GONE MISSING

BASED ON A TRUE STORY

SONNY BREWER

MACADAM CAGE

MacAdam/Cage
155 Sansome Street, Suite 550
San Francisco, CA 94104
Copyright © Sonny Brewer 2007

ISBN 978-1-59692-061-3

Manufactured in the United States of America

Book and jacket design by Dorothy Carico Smith

FOR REX THE WONDER DOG AND CORMAC,

THE ALPHA AND OMEGA MALES

OF THE DOGS IN MY LIFE

AUTHOR'S NOTE

WHEN MY CELL PHONE RANG, I saw from the caller ID that it was my house sitter. I'll call him Drew. I was in San Francisco, on the other side of the country. "Man, your dog is missing," Drew said. "I can't find Cormac anywhere."

I was completely silent.

Drew asked me what to do. "I don't know," I said.

I would not be home for another week and a half. As Cormac remained missing, those days poured out for me slowly, like cold blackstrap molasses. This story is based on the real events that followed—and some that preceded— that awful phone call.

Some of the facts are changed because I waited three years to write this and I forgot some details. Reporters are forgiven when they change small nonessential details; "hazards of memory" is the official excuse. A blue coffee cup might become a red coffee cup in an article. When I wrote that I picked out my puppy from a litter of puppies, I truly could not—and cannot now—remember whether there were five puppies or seven puppies in that litter, and how many were sisters and how many were brothers.

When I began this book, I could not—and cannot now—remember whether or not my brother and my sister were with me at my grandmother's house on that certain weekend long ago. I decided to leave them out of the telling. My wife and my children, however, are with me here on these pages. We keep our names. The dogs keep their names.

My fortune cookie at a Chinese restaurant advised me to live out of my imagination, not out of my memory. In this book I have done that. I think of Huck Finn telling us that we did not know him unless we'd read Mr. Mark Twain's *The Adventures of Tom Sawyer*. "There was things which he stretched," Huck said, "but mainly he told the truth. That is nothing. I never seen anybody but lied one time or another..." Same here.

In *Writers at Work, The Paris Review Interviews, Volume 8*, John Irving said he'd never been able to keep a diary or write a memoir. "I've tried," he said. "I begin by telling the truth, by remembering real people, relatives, and friends. The landscape detail is pretty good, but the people aren't quite interesting enough—they don't have quite enough to do with one another; of course, what unsettles me and bores me is the absence of plot. And so I find a little something that I exaggerate, a little; gradually I have an autobiography on the way to becoming a lie. The lie, of course, is more interesting."

While there are stretchers in here, and a little exaggeration now and again, I must say that "mainly I've told the truth" in this story of losing my good dog Cormac.

So, if you think you see yourself here, but you believe you are certainly thinner or smarter than I've described, remember: this is a dog's tale, and any resemblance to persons alive or dead is purely coincidental, unless otherwise intended.

PROLOGUE

IT ALL BEGAN with a silver and black-saddled German Shepherd. He was my first dog.

I remember it this way:

The big dog leaned all its weight against my leg. I answered by reaching out my hand to stroke the thick fur between his ears, looking into his deep mahogany eyes. He knew something was wrong, but I had no confidence to share. I turned up my face and searched my mother's eyes hoping to find some reassurance.

She repeated her instructions, telling me to take a different school bus, telling me not to come home this afternoon on bus 50, to instead find bus 64 and show the driver the note she had just tucked into my shirt pocket. I placed my hand over the pocket, as if to press the note into the skin of my chest so I would not lose it somewhere around school or on the playground.

The only time I had ever been to Big Mama's creepy house was when my father had taken me there, and never had I spent the night there. It had a woodshake roof going mossy green and gray walls with no paint. Almost all of my relatives and friends now had a television. She did not even have a radio. Plus, she smelled like the snuff she dipped, or she smelled like wood smoke from the black iron stove in her kitchen. She was also huge, her bosom like a fat pillow, and it seemed to me that I should not call her big to her face. My father had hit me across the face for calling Waymon Culpepper by his first name. And this seemed to me a worse thing to say, that my grandmother was big.

And, she was not my mama.

"Who's going to feed Rex, Mother?" I looked at my dog and his eyes brightened and his tail wagged, but tentatively.

"I will feed your dog, Sonny. Or your daddy will."

"No. You have to feed Rex," I demanded. "You feed him, or I'm not going on the other bus."

"Young man! You will not speak to me like that," she said, making fists and propping them on her hips. Then her face went soft and she pushed her fingers through her hair. "Sonny, sweetie, don't worry about Rex. I will feed him."

"But why do I have to go to her house?"

"It is not *her* house. She's your grandmother," mother said. My father required me to address her as Big Mama. I think that's because she used to be married to my Pop Brewer, and "Grammy" was used by Pop Brewer's new wife. "Look, Sonny, Big Mama's excited to have you come for the weekend. *Why* you're going is so your father and I can—well, take a break from things. Maybe drive to the lake. Just talk."

"You mean argue?"

"No, Sonny. And I don't like you saying that. This is a good idea, good for all of us. You stay tonight and tomorrow night at Big Mama's house. Your daddy and I will come and get you on Sunday morning. We'll all stay for lunch, and we'll come home. It's not like you're being sent to a work camp, for goodness sake."

"But, Mother…"

"Rex will be fine. You just be sure to get on the right bus. Mr. Owens drives bus 64. He told me himself that he will watch after you on his bus."

"I'm eleven years old. I don't need anybody to watch me."

"Of course, you don't, Sonny. It's just that one of those Rayford boys picked a fight on that bus last week."

"I'm not afraid of Doug Rayford," I snapped.

"No, I don't expect you are." She tousled my hair and told me to go and meet my bus. "I hear it coming down the road. Better hurry."

I stopped on the top step of the porch, the morning sun warming my face in the frosty air. I squatted and put down my books and Rex nuzzled my chest. I still could not believe, after almost six months, that he was my very own dog. He wagged his tail and licked my face. I laughed and turned my face to avoid his wet tongue. I heard the bus's brakes screech at the Dawkins' house just around the bend. I hugged Rex, grabbed my books, and jumped up. I told Rex to stay, and ran down the hill to meet the yellow bus.

My grandmother did not have a phone. And so I did not learn until Sunday morning that Rex had not eaten since I left.

"If there was any doubt that Rex is your dog, and your dog alone, it's all gone now," my mother told me.

My father had not come with her to Big Mama's.

"That dog sat watching for the school bus the way he always does, and when it went right on past he made like he was going to chase it down. He lay in the yard until dark, watching the highway." My mother said Rex refused the bowl of food she took out to him, that he walked away from her standing there and went underneath the house.

"Three times yesterday I looked under the house, and there he lay," my mother told me. "I'd call him, and he'd raise his head to look at me, but he wouldn't budge." I sat with the two women, listening to Mama, looking at her as though she told of a hole that opened up in the ground.

"Well, I'll declare. I reckon I'd forget my head if it wasn't attached," Big Mama said, pushing her chair back from the table. She got up and took a dish towel from a wooden peg beneath the windowsill. She folded the threadbare cloth into a kind of potholder and, letting down the oven door, wrapped it around the handle of a heavy iron skillet. She took out the pan of cornbread and set it onto the table atop a jar lid that served as a trivet. She left the towel wrapped around the skillet handle and eased down into her chair with a *hmmph* and a smile.

"Now," said Big Mama, "let's say the blessing." And we bowed our heads and she addressed God in a clear voice, thanking him, and asking him, "…to keep things about the way they are, if you please." I did not close my eyes, and my eyebrows were locked together in a frown.

As soon as *amen* was spoken I entreated my mother to tell me more about Rex.

"Nothing more to tell, really, Sonny. He's upset, I guess, that you aren't there. And I reckon he'll be fine as soon as you are."

"But Rex didn't eat since Friday. He's not fine. Can we just go home?"

"Sonny, let me say something," Big Mama said, spreading butter on a slice of cornbread. She put down the knife and the triangle of hot cornbread. She folded her hands in her lap and drew me into the warmth of her gaze. She spoke my name again. I think my troubled face might've softened some, but my eyes were still full.

Big Mama had walked and talked all day yesterday, asking me a thousand questions that I answered, and she had told me a thousand things about the *homeplace*, as she called her house and land. She had pointed out trees my father had claimed and climbed. She told me of the bull that chased her from the feeding pen just last Christmas, and that she bonged the beast on the head with her bucket.

She told how much she missed Mister Frank, as she called her husband who was like my grandfather only not really kin to me. "I can nearly about feel Mister Frank on these cool autumn evenings, 'specially at twilight when whippoorwills venture to call out from the darkening woods yonder across them hills and hollows," Big Mama had said, pointing a crooked finger south toward the treeline a mile distant. She asked me, did Daddy still make those long hauls to the West Coast? I told her yes. It did not register with me then that we had not visited her since the middle of summer.

"That's where Daddy found my dog. Out in California," I said. "Where Hollywood is. That's how he came up with a famous dog like Rex." I told my grandmother that my father had brought me the dog last summer. "Daddy told me Rex is the grandson of Rex the Wonder

Dog. From the movies, you know," I said, my eyebrows high. I told her I only knew about Rex the Wonder Dog in the comic books, but Daddy had told me this was the movie dog's grandson.

"Did you see Rex the Wonder Dog in the movies, Big Mama?"

She had only laughed and said, "Lord, no, son. Mister Frank and I were too busy running this farm to get to a picture show." She had stopped walking abruptly then, looking across the pasture toward where Mud Creek cut through a stand of willows. "We did go off to town one Saturday night—you must've been a baby then—and saw a silly picture about a talking mule. Francis, the thing was called. I never saw Mister Frank laugh so, but then he reckoned money was too hard to get to spend it on such a trifle. And we never went back." She dusted her hands on her dress, turned back toward the house. "We might ought to have gone to another picture show, it seems," she said, and had picked up her pace, walking ahead of me.

Now she got up and went to the counter and got the apples she'd peeled earlier. She stopped and looked out the window, but I didn't think she saw a thing. Some of the same sadness I'd seen yesterday flickered in Big Mama's eyes as she leaned close to the table, setting down the dish of apple slices. "We had a big mutt here on the farm, part shepherd and part bloodhound of all things. Ugliest dog I ever saw. But he was Mister Frank's favorite. Called him Grizzle." She sat down and looked at me, not blinking, completely ignoring my mother at the table. She put her hands on either side of her plate. "Lord, son, I hope I'm wrong, but I'm of a mind your dog is an old-timer and he has gone down in his back."

"Big Mama!" Mother scolded. "Why in the world would you tell this child such a thing?"

"Because his sorry daddy won't, that's why. I'm just saying that Grizzle…"

"What? Big Mama, what?" I began to cry and shook my head. "I told you, Mother, I shouldn't go away from my dog!"

"For heaven's sake. Both of you, please…"

"You have to know, Sonny, if Rex is down it is nothing you did. You hear me, son? Coming to see your granny wasn't part of this. When Grizzle got down, Mister Frank told me it was a fault of the Shepherd in him. Their long backs don't bear up well as they get older."

"Rex is not *older*," I shouted, and leaped from the table, tipping over my chair. I ran from the room as Mother said, "Good Lord, Big Mama! This just beats all! I'll just have to get him home now if he doesn't run off through the woods on foot. Why would you do this, Marjene? Is this how you pay back a boy's affection?"

*

As I think back, I know now that the old woman did not get up to follow her daughter-in-law out of the kitchen, where the beans and corn and squash still sat steaming in their bowls.

She would have waited until she heard the automobile's tires leave the gravel of her drive to meet the quiet pavement before she would have put her napkin over the uneaten potatoes on her plate and pushed back her glass of sweet tea, its few ice cubes near melted. I'm glad Big Mama did not have a telephone to get the news that Rex had to be put down. It would be a long time before another visit, and the story would have acquired some measure of peace before it was told to her that Daddy had held out the gun to me, offering me the shot that would take my paralyzed dog out of his misery.

Daddy's face had been a mess of anger, blurred in my vision that focused on the fat blue pistol in his hand, its wood handle extended toward me. He had not stopped scowling since I crawled out from beneath the house, dirty and huffing from dragging Rex on a bed sheet into the sunlight that made him close his eyes.

"He's your'n, boy," Daddy had said, still holding the butt of the gun toward me, and I'd looked straight at him like he was a copperhead in a coil, that if I broke the stare I'd be struck. Big Mama would learn that when he asked me flat out, "You want to shoot him?" that I'd said no and squeezed hard as I could to keep from crying. "Then move. Get over here back of me."

And when I stepped to the side, Rex blinked his eyes open and locked on mine, looking for reassurance. Somebody might tell Big Mama how I gave in and cried then, but they wouldn't know to tell her how that river of bewilderment and anger flowed right from me into the silent, waiting eyes of Rex the Wonder Dog, when what he needed was confidence. But I had none to share.

ONE

I WAS A BOY in the low red-clay hills of middle Alabama. Today, at fifty-something, I make my home on the Gulf Coast. And if I tell you it's in a "small town in Alabama" that I live (or in Mississippi, Tennessee, or Georgia, for that matter), you may think of pickup trucks with big tires and camouflage paint, guns in the back window.

Don't think that.

Not this time.

When I say Fairhope is a small town in Alabama, think of art galleries and coffee shops and cafés and sailboats bobbing at anchor on Mobile Bay, beneath the high bluff upon which the town is perched. Think of flowers on the corners of brick-paved sidewalks, gnarly live oaks draped with Spanish moss, magnolias and tall pines swaying in waterfront breezes that smell faintly of fish and salt. Think of a bustling independent bookstore on the corner; and think of my sleepy bookstore with old and rare volumes just down the street. Think of twelve thousand residents and more published writers per capita than any other place in the country. Think of a new library that is the centerpiece of the town's architecture.

Now think about the world's handsomest and sweetest Golden Retriever, as smart as any four-year-old child, who answers to the name Cormac, and who lives on the outskirts of Fairhope in an aging farmhouse on an easy hill, with two acres to roam, complete with a barn and swimming pool. Think of what a great place this is from which to launch a red-haired dog's bizarre adventure, which actually began with a brown and white dog just before Cormac came along.

*

If I had been thinking about the screwy nature of the little Jack Russell beside me, Zebbie, I'd have grabbed his collar as soon as I saw the aging pedestrian with her Peekapoo on its leash. Even by the coiled-spring standard of the breed, Zebbie was over-endowed with the *sproing* factor.

But I was lost in thought, my Jeep's window down, rolling along the street at a good clip. By the time I registered what might happen, the deed was already in motion. When we passed the lady and her dog, Zebbie rocked back on his haunches and launched out the window of my Jeep. Too quick for me to stop him. I slammed on my brakes, relieved no cars were behind me, and looked into the rearview mirror: Zebbie tumbled down the sidewalk like some bizarre living bowling ball in a Tim Burton movie.

By the time I had curbed the Jeep and raced on foot back to the scene, Zebbie had squared off, yapping at the lady who now had her little dog crushed to her bosom. She screamed at her attacker, then at me. I grabbed Zebbie, who tried to bite me. I apologized over and over, even though my dog had not made contact—physical, that is—with either the woman or her fluffy pet. After she took my name and phone number, I made a hasty exit. My hands were shaking as I put Zebbie on the seat of the Jeep and looked him over. I rolled up the window and drove to my vet's office.

Belle—Dr. St. Clair to most of her clients—gave Zeb a good checkup, found nothing busted, lectured me briefly, and released us to continue to the bookstore. I looked over my shoulder twice as I fumbled with the keys to the shop, making sure the little Terrier was still in "sit" on the sidewalk right behind me. Zebbie sat, his black eyes shining like ball bearings, his head cocked to the side, curious about the jangle of keys. This first small act of opening the store for business was, for him, an engaging mystery.

I was still shaken. I looked at Zebbie again to make

sure no blood had sprung a leak, no bones were trying to poke through the skin. His brown and white coat was as beautiful as a puppy's fresh from a basket on Christmas morning. At two years, Zebbie was no puppy, but he still behaved or *mis*behaved like an inexperienced youngster. I couldn't believe the dog was unmarked and emotionally oblivious, it seemed, to his close call with disaster.

"You keeping banker's hours these days?" Someone yelled at me from a passing car. I turned to see Drew Bilden's truck stopped in the middle of the street, the passenger glass rolled down, Drew leaning toward the open window. "Can I get a job with you if I decide to give up real work?"

"Stop by later," I said. "I have a story to tell you." I hooked my thumb toward Zebbie. "You won't believe what this silly dog did on the way to the store this morning. I'll have some coffee going in fifteen minutes."

"I'll bring a résumé." Drew sat upright in his seat, as if considering the street beyond his windshield. The electric window slid upward, then stopped. "You still thinking about getting rid of the Terrier?"

"I don't know." I looked down at the Jack Russell, thought of how I really wanted this to work out. But, just two weeks ago I had told Drew about Zebbie eating the cover of a rare leatherbound first edition of *From Manassas to Appomattox* by General James Longstreet. An overlooked case open behind the counter and in ten minutes Zebbie had reduced the book's value from $5,000 to a couple hundred dollars after repairs. "You know," I had said to Drew, massaging my forehead while bemusedly appraising the dog, "I told Zebbie 'three strikes and you're out.' That was twenty strikes back."

And then today's stunt—another definite swing and a miss.

"Are you a candidate to take him?" I wanted to know.

"Free?" Drew asked.

"I'm sure we could work out something. Something mutually beneficial."

"Right," Drew said. "You don't fool me."

I smiled and took the key from the lock and dropped it into my jacket pocket and opened the bright red French door to Over the Transom Bookstore. It squeaked on its hinges, and Zebbie gave an impatient yip. He ran quickly past me to make sure there were no burglars lurking in the bookstore. The little dog performed this morning ritual with great verve and authority.

Stepping across the threshold, I was greeted by the pleasant musky smell of aged literature. Not all of the books on my shelves would pass for literature, but those other volumes were in purposeful minority. Each old book in the store, whatever its title, lent its particular fragrance to the air swirled about by the dusty paddles of six ancient ceiling fans. For me, the conjure of the myriad authors' words was thus made palpable and given direct access through my nose to all my other senses.

I walked past the sales counter and turned on the computer. While the Toshiba got ready to toss me some emails and, hopefully, an order or two from my online catalog of used and rare books, I went to the small kitchen in the back of the store and made a pot of coffee.

I took down a book from the shelves behind the counter where I kept special orders and valuable or otherwise interesting volumes I wished to research. This one, *Gombo Zhebes—Little Dictionary of Creole Proverbs* by Lafcadio Hearn, was from a small collection I'd purchased. I'd looked it up in the price guidebook at the end of the day yesterday. As a true first edition, published in 1885, it was valued at $500. Maybe Pierre Fouchere, fellow shopkeeper, friend, and bibliophile, whose store featured old records and baseball cards, would stop by the bookstore today. He claimed a Creole heritage and had told me to let him know whenever I got such books.

I typed the publication information and a detailed description of the book's flaws and strengths into the appropriate fields on my computer screen, established my selling price of $500, and clicked SUBMIT.

I put the book into a glass case, closed the door, and walked back to the kitchen and poured myself a cup of

coffee in a ceramic mug, a large white one with a silhou-
ette skyline of the Big Apple with the twin towers still
standing. I heard the bell ring announcing a customer
had entered the store. I stirred sugar into my coffee and
walked to the front of the store to find Drew scratching
Zebbie's head.

"Can I get you a cup of coffee?" I asked.

"Real men drink their coffee between six and seven
in the morning," Drew said. He looked at his watch. "But
okay. When in Rome, I suppose." We walked to the
kitchen, talking about the recent run of good weather in
Fairhope. I poured Drew a cup, and we went back to the
front of the store. "So what did the little monster do this
time?" Drew asked, gesturing toward Zebbie with his
coffee cup.

"Well, I'm clocking down Morphy Avenue at maybe
thirty-five. Windows down on the Jeep, Zebbie with his
head out getting his fix. Same parts in the same play he and
I have acted out along a hundred miles of streets in this
town on a hundred other days. Walking down the sidewalk, meeting us, came a lady and her doggie on a leash."

"Oh, no! Don't tell me."

"He jumped out the window," I said.

"What did you do, man?"

"After I got him back in the Jeep, I took him to the vet.
Belle said he wasn't injured."

"Did she yell at you?"

"More like shook her finger at me."

"Yep, she's a crusader about that. Keeps her dogs on some kind of clever leash thing in the bed of her truck. I thought about that arrangement of hers the other day when I saw a construction worker's dog riding on his toolbox lid at sixty miles an hour, barking at every car he met. I couldn't believe the Labrador's agility and balance, dancing side to side of the truck at that speed."

"I'd never let a dog do that," I said. "That's the way you carpenters behave."

"Yeah, you just launch 'em out the car window."

Both of us looked at Zebbie on the windowsill. He was sound asleep. He looked like an angel dog. "Look at that," I said with a sigh. "Now *that's* the picture I imagined when I brought him home." As if in contrary response, Zebbie woke up and bounced down, rounded the counter. "He really is a good dog."

"Right," Drew drank from his cup, looked over his shoulder, and said. "Then why's he peeing on those books over there?"

I jumped up from my stool, spilling coffee. "What? Where?"

But then I saw him, his leg hiked, a healthy stream washing down books on a bottom shelf on the other side of the room. "Zebbie!" The little dog looked over his

shoulder, beaming satisfaction, and continued his business, then ran back to me, his tail wagging. "Zeb!" I yelled.
"That's it. Last strike. Last straw." I scowled. Zebbie smiled.

"That's not fair."

"You want him? Dog house, dog bed, leash, bowl,
brush, chew toys. One price for all. Absolutely free."

"What about Diana and the kids?"

"The dad giveth and the dad taketh away," I said.

Drew knelt to pet Zebbie. "Do you think he could
ride a toolbox?"

"Like he's bolted down," I said, and then looked at
Drew. I had not, until then, taken my smoldering eyes
from Zebbie. "You're not going to do that, right?"

"Oh, give me a break," Drew said. "Besides," he continued, "Linda's probably not going to let him go anywhere with me. She's asked me a thousand times if
Zebbie's up for grabs yet."

"Don't put it like that," I said.

"I didn't. Linda did. She said she knew right away
this dog wouldn't last with you. Said you two were like a
jalapeño and a glass of milk." Drew stood up with Zebbie
curled into the crook of his muscled forearm. "You've got
this catch-and-release thing going. Dogs and people,
man, is about *rapport*. Look that word up, Bookstore
Man, after you tell me when I can get Zebulon's things."

TWO

"YOU DID WHAT?" Diana poured for herself a glass of red wine. The boys, John Luke and Dylan, were outside shooting hoops, caught up enough in their play that they didn't notice Zebbie was not with me. I'd parked out front, leaving the driveway clear around the basketball goal and avoiding for a spell their questions about the dog.

"I gave him to Drew," I said. "I made a mistake with Zebbie." Leaning against the kitchen counter, still holding a book I'd brought home from the store, I grew quiet and looked at the floor.

"You should have thought about his background a little, don't you think, Sonny? You got him from an old man who raised him for two years while living alone. Plus, he's a Jack Russell."

Diana poured a second glass of wine and handed it to me. "The silly mutt jumped out of the car window," I said, "on the way to the bookstore this morning."

"What?"

"Oh, he's fine. Belle checked him out, and Drew will

keep an eye on him. Those two are a good match." I sipped the cabernet, then held the glass away and tilted it, watching the wine creep nearer the rim. Diana knew I was distracted, and not really thinking about Zebbie. She moved a barstool to the end of the kitchen counter and sat down.

"So, it's not getting any better with walk-ins at the bookstore?" she asked, going straight to the bigger thing on my mind, as she often does. It's a gift she has possessed since we first dated.

"No, and what's worse, internet orders have slowed to a trickle," I said.

"What's with that?"

"Oh, too many mom-and-pops posting used books from their mobile homes in Minnesota or Paris, for that matter," I said, and added, "from double-wides on the banks of the Seine." I smiled.

She asked me if I really thought home booksellers were enough competition to affect storefront operations like Over the Transom. "I do," I said. "They don't have the overhead, and it seems each new online seller puts his prices a little below the market. It's kind of a mess. Good thing you've got a real job."

"Well, maybe things will turn around soon for the better. Let's hope so," Diana said. "Do you think," she asked, her voice quiet, her eyes on me, "that's partly why you gave up on Zebbie?"

"I didn't give up," I said. "I got fed up."

"I understand," she said. "And I agree that Drew and Zebbie will get along just fine." She drew invisible shapes on the countertop with her finger. "So we might as well go ahead and tell the boys that Drew now has Zebbie." Diana said.

"You think I should've called for a family powwow before handing him off to Drew?"

"No," she said, "They weren't bonded with him. We've talked about that before. You'll be fair and honest with them. That's all they need. It will be a little hard for them. It's hard for you, too."

My face relaxed. Diana picked up her wineglass and swirled the dark red liquid, watching the little fingers run down the inside of the glass.

"I can't believe what I'm about to say." She shook her head. "Maybe you could soften the blow by telling the boys we'll get a new puppy. Right away. We can start looking as soon as we decide together, as a family, just what kind."

"We've talked about that," I said. "One reason we gave Zeb a try was because he was already housebroke. Puppies chew and whine all night and pee on the floor and poop in the corner."

"All of that?" Diana asked.

"And more."

"Right," she said. "And some of the more is the love the boys and you and I will toss into the mix."

I took the wineglass from Diana's hand, put it on the counter and wrapped her in my arms. "A puppy's going to be a pain in the neck. Just so you know and there'll be no yelling at me when a chair leg gets chewed off."

"*You* are often a pain in the neck."

"I'll be expected to clean up the mess, I suppose," I said.

"Thereby setting a great example for your sons, who will help out." Diana said.

"Maybe this new doggie," I said, lighting up, "will show me where the bone of great riches is buried. Teach an old bookseller some new trick."

"You don't need a dog to show you where your fortunes are hidden," Diana said. "We both have a good idea where you need to dig."

I knew Diana was talking about the novel I'd been writing. She read each new chapter as I finished it. She told me it was a good book, that I would find a publisher. "If I could believe it the way you do," I said.

"You will," she said. I felt a small lift, like some kite winging up just before a pine tree branch snagged it from the sky. She walked to the door, held it open for me. We stepped outside into the remainder of a warm day.

"Boys…" I called, letting my voice trail off as I noticed a first star winking in the twilight's fading of the sun.

THREE

"DOES DADDY ASK the computer everything, Mommy?" asked little Dylan. "How does the computer know about our dog, Mommy? Will it show us a picture?"

Moments earlier, sitting in the family room talking about the idea of getting a puppy, Diana and John Luke had giggled when I suggested asking the computer for help. Now they gathered around me at the computer in the study as I typed a question into the search engine, then sat back from the screen. "Okay, guys, I did a search for the most family-friendly dog." Even a glimpse at the page of matches revealed the first choice for families and kids: Golden Retriever.

"Does it show us our dog?" Dylan asked.

"Well, son, the all-knowing computer…" I said, pausing for effect. My histrionics drew from Diana a roll of her eyes. "The oracle here tells your mom and me that we probably want to get a Golden Retriever. You guys look here. Here are some pictures of Goldens."

John Luke leaned in close. "Some are dark and some

are light," he said. "There's one that's almost white." He pointed to a pair of goldens on the webpage. The one on the right had a Scandinavian blond coat.

"Do they get *big*?" Diana asked, a frown forming.

"Let's see," I said. "Says here 75 pounds or so."

"Or *so*?"

"That's the upper limit in the weight range. But nothing says our dog will get as big as it possibly can."

"Okay," she said, "we're getting a big dog."

"It starts off little," I corrected, holding my palms six inches apart.

"Daddy's funny, right, Mom?" Dylan asked.

"Only sometimes," Diana answered. And with that we set upon our mission to acquire a Golden Retriever. When John Luke wanted to know, would we find a dog on the internet? I said no. "We'll do this the old-fashioned way. Which means—ah, I don't know what it means." I rocked back in the chair pushing it away from the desk, my fingers laced behind my head. I looked at Diana. "I cannot believe this."

"What?"

"It dawns on me, here and now, that I have never been shopping for a puppy. Diana," I said, as if discovering my toes were webbed, "I have never owned a puppy."

"Are you *sure*? Never is a long time for an old guy like you."

It was as if I hadn't heard a word she'd said. "I've never owned a puppy," I said. "All the dogs in my life…"

"Well," Diana added, "it's not like there have been thousands."

"No. But there have been *some*." I thought of the Basset Hound I'd handed off to my Aunt Lillian when I was in college. I thought of the Labrador mix I found after the Navy and gave to a woman who lived alone on a farm near my mother.

Diana stepped closer, taking Dylan's hand. "Mommy's never had a puppy either."

I socked John Luke on the arm, and hopped to my feet. "There you have it," I said. "We'll get a puppy. But right now let's get pizza!"

We piled into my Jeep, talking all the way to the restaurant about getting our new doggy. On the drive home from Benny's Pizza Shop, with the boys occupied in the backseat, I told her it still bugged me how easily the boys had given in to Zebbie's new home with Drew.

"Well, the boys know Drew, and they both like him and Linda to visit," Diana said. She told me that John Luke had asked her if Drew would bring Zebbie to visit sometime. "The way Dylan put it," she said, "was, 'Can we borrow Zebbie if we want to, Mommy?'"

Still, it seemed to me, I said to Diana, that they were *over it, man*. I had even mentioned to Drew how quickly the boys let Zebbie slip from their lives. He'd repeated his belief that we didn't have rapport with Zebbie. Drew had preached, "Y'all didn't have it with the Zebulon. I do. Linda does. You were simply an instrument, brother, in the universal intent to set things right. Get over it. Move on."

Diana and I talked on the drive home and mostly she agreed with Drew. "Zebbie was a surprise when you brought him home. We'll all be in on this one together," she said, "and we can do some things differently." We agreed that our poor experience with Zebbie living indoors, the new dog would be an outside dog. I suggested installing a dog door on the screened back porch, effectively eliminating the need for a doghouse. "With liberal inside visitation," Diana offered.

"That should suit everyone," I agreed.

The backyard was already fenced, but when we got home, even though it was the dark of night, I took my flashlight and announced I would go outside and double-check for low spots where a pup might be able to get out. Diana and Dylan plopped down at the kitchen table, while John Luke switched on the television.

The backyard was quiet as I walked slowly along the fencerow, training the flashlight beam on the bottom of the chain-link fabric. I wanted to let my mind settle. It had been another slow day in the bookstore. I'd sold only three books all day.

An owl called from a dark treetop somewhere very near, and I switched off my light. Three blocks away another owl answered. I looked up, but could see nothing, only tree branches and deep shadows. I wondered, would the owl almost directly above me go to the other? Or would the other leave its branch and wing on over this way? For ten minutes I stood in the dark listening to the exchange between the pair until, finally, the more distant bird ceased to answer.

"Too bad, old man," I said. I turned on my light and completed my survey, satisfied the new dog would stay in the fenced yard. Then I walked to the corner of the yard where there were no trees. I switched off the light and waited for my eyes to adjust to the darkness. I looked up at a million stars, pinholes in a black cape draped over the world. I waited for a moment in the quiet. When I was standing at the back door ready to go inside, the owl from off in the night decided to get back on line. The close one responded right away. "I guess that's one for not giving up," I muttered, then opened the door into the kitchen. There, on the table warmed by the room's yellow light, lay Dylan's coloring book, open. His crayons were scattered about on the table. I looked at his handiwork, and was closing the book when I saw the freehand drawing he'd done on the inside front cover. It was a big red dog.

FOUR

HIS FATHER'S NAME was Rock. His grandfather's name was Bear. When the man on the phone told me this, I was encouraged. I was searching for a rugged but good-looking male, and this could be just the place to get our Golden Retriever puppy, a fellow we might name King. I knew the naming of the pup would be a challenge. Diana and the boys and I had been known to pour ourselves into hot debates on lesser matters. I thought with a chuckle that I could always suggest we Google a list of names.

On the other hand, Diana and John Luke and Dylan and I had all given a unanimous nod to a Golden for the family dog, so there was a fair hope of agreement on a name. Whatever the dog's name finally, a Rock and a Bear should add some manly gristle and good looks to the gene pool.

"And you don't run a puppy farm, right?" The man on the phone told me no.

"Come on out to the house," he said. "You'll see my dogs, and you'll be satisfied I'm telling the truth." His voice reminded me of Wilford Brimley, with some Garrison Keillor nuances. "We've got four puppies left. Two boys and two girls."

He hadn't said two males and two females. His pups were boys and girls. That was good, I thought. I told the man on the phone that I'd load up my family and come to see his young Golden Retrievers the next day.

On Saturday morning, I asked Pierre to mind the bookstore for a bit, something Pierre had repeatedly offered to do. He seemed not to mind leaving his own store under part-time supervision. "I'll swap stores with you, if you want," Pierre often joked.

"One of these days," I said, "I might surprise you and take you up on it. So don't offer lightly, *mon ami.*"

I had my coffee, then paid a visit to Belle, who warned me to be patient as I looked for a dog. She said Goldens are so popular they're often overbred, and many are too lean and look more like short Irish Setters.

"A good Golden will be blocky and muscular," Belle told me. "What you'd expect a fine Lab to look like, with a handsome square head and a strong muzzle." I told her I'd found the son of a Rock, the grandson of a Bear. She laughed and told me it sounded promising.

I went by the bookstore and talked to Pierre for a few minutes. He'd lost the password to the computer. I wrote it on a note card and taped it to the counter underneath the laptop. While I was doing this, he said he thought I should take a couple years' break before getting another dog. "It's not for me," I said. "It'll be a family pet."

"Sure thing," he said, nodding, his eyebrows raised.

"Besides," I said, "it could take two years to find the right dog." He shook his head, and walked me to the door. I drove home to pick up Diana and the boys. We all piled into the Jeep and drove toward Bay Minette, a small town twenty miles north of Fairhope. Diana held the driving directions.

"You know," I said, as we got closer to our destination, "I had sure hoped we'd find a puppy through a reference from someone we know, not though a classified ad."

"But all our referrals we got came from people whose Goldens look more like Setters, and you said Belle said…"

"I know. But this seems so, so…"

"Like shopping for a used sofa," Diana offered.

"Exactly."

"Well, let's just have a look. A look won't hurt."

"No," I said. I was silent for a moment. "But, you know, looking for a puppy should be that: *looking*. We haven't looked at a single pup, Diana. We've just been talking," I complained.

"Just relax," she said. "Life is good."

"If this is a puppy farm…"

"Sonny!"

"Sorry, honey," I said. "Isn't this my turn coming up?"

Diana nodded, and I turned onto an unpaved side road of smoothly packed crushed white oyster shells. It was a comfortable ride up the long drive, lined with pruned azalea bushes and young live oaks. We wound our way up a low hill to a two-story brick colonial with white columns. An ebony black Chevy Silverado gleamed on a concrete parking pad.

"Not the *Deliverance* setting you were imagining, huh?" Diana asked.

"Whatever I imagined," I said, "it wasn't this."

An old man walked around the corner of the house followed by a prancing and beautiful dark-red Golden Retriever, obviously the mother, her quartet of puppies wending and stumbling at her feet. The man wore faded jeans, boots, and a cowboy shirt not tucked in. He pinched off a piece of biscuit he was eating and handed it to the mama dog. He ruffled the fur on her head.

"How do, folks? You've come to look at my pups, I reckon."

"Yes, sir," I said, my eyes on the puppies, not the man.

"Tell them boys to come on up here," the man said. "You got to get the little ones together with the little ones to get this right."

Diana and I exchanged looks, smiled, and nodded to

the boys, who clearly understood they were being given a special invitation. John Luke and Dylan rushed forward and dropped to their knees. All four puppies surrounded them. The man in the cowboy shirt stepped forward and extended his hand. "My name's Jack Bennett."

"I'm Sonny Brewer. This is my wife, Diana."

"Pleased to meet you, ma'am." He nodded to me, "Sir." Then Mr. Bennett turned his attention to the dogs and the boys rolling and giggling on the grass with puppies all over them. Mr. Bennett approached the mama dog. She wrapped her body around his leg and leaned her entire weight against him.

"Look at that," I declared to Diana.

"What?" she asked. "Where?"

"At the mother dog. I swear she smiled."

"Of course, she's smiling," Mr. Bennett said. "She doesn't always. When she does, you can be sure she okays the adoption." I decided this was *not* a puppy farm where dogs are merely inventory. This man's dogs were about as close to family as four-leggeds could get.

"You know how it goes when you wade through a litter of puppies?" Mr. Bennett asked. "How one little guy's tail is wagging just for you? You step back. He follows. You take a side step, he follows."

"I could see that," I said.

"Don't look now, but there's a reddish-brown pup

who's been shadowing you since you stepped out of that vehicle of yours…" I was surprised when I looked at the ground near my feet and saw the puppy there.

"Now, that's what you call bonding, Mr. Brewer. I don't often see it that pure and natural. No, sir, not many times."

The adoption seemed fated. I dropped down on my knees and patted my thighs. The puppy was a ball of fur the color of Ann-Margret's hair in those movies where it was between red and auburn. He crawled immediately into my lap. Diana got the attention of our sons. She pointed to me snuggling with the nipping, wiggling pup. John Luke and Dylan glanced quickly at their playmates, and, realizing they had not singled out one puppy from the others, ran to join me.

"Want me to get your checkbook, Sonny?" Diana leaned against the fender of the Jeep, her arms crossed, a smile for me.

"Oh, *I* have to pay? I thought maybe—ah…"

"That I'd buy lunch? Sure," Diana said.

"Better take what you can get there," Mr. Bennett said, his eyes twinkling. "A dog'll sometimes rob your bank, you know."

"Okay," I said. "My checkbook's in the glove compartment. I've got a pen." I picked up the little dog. His mother came to investigate. She decided I made the grade, I guess, because she smiled up at me as I held her boy, then walked away to join her other children. The puppy had longish legs that dangled below my forearm. He turned his head and began chewing on my whiskers. His breath was hard, like a cigar smoker's, but his honey-brown eyes fended off criticism. Maybe he was practicing his chewing technique for the furniture at our place, or, he could be hungry. I knew that I was ready for a nice lunch, and asked, "Do I get to pick where we eat?"

"Anywhere at all," Diana said.

I put the pup down and wrote the check, while Mr. Bennett filled out the AKC forms for his registration. I had not even thought about the pedigree, said I didn't think I'd file the papers, that it wasn't important to me. Mr. Bennett suggested otherwise, made the point that it helped track the dog if another owner should acquire "this fellow."

"No, sir. Not a chance. No one else acquires this fellow but the welcoming ground at the end of his long life."

"It's your choice, of course, to register him or not. And I do hope it works out that you two never part company," Mr. Bennett said.

"Look," I said. "Can there be any doubt we are made for each other?" The little dog had sat when I put him down and hadn't moved since. He just stared up at me with his pink tongue hanging out.

On our ride home, Diana motioned with her head toward the backseat, where the boys and the puppy were all in a tangle with each other, laughing and squealing.

"Yes," I said, a few miles later, "this dog, excuse me— this *fellow*—is one of the family. He's a keeper no matter what." At a stop sign, before taking off again, I turned and looked at the puppy in the back seat. John Luke and Dylan were now sedate and looking out their side windows. The young Golden, maybe twenty pounds at three months, was stretched out between the two boys, completely still, with his muzzle down on the seat but his eyes wide open. He looked straight at me, and I was so captured in his gaze that I didn't see the car pull up behind me at the stop sign. The driver in the car behind me blew his horn, and I got underway again.

"You know," I said, "we talked about naming him King. Be we can't just settle for King. That could be any old king. But Cormac as in Cormac Mac Art, who ruled County Meath in the third century and was 'wise, learned, valiant, and mild.' Now that's a kingly name."

"Now, how can you know such a piece of trivia? You made that up, Sonny Brewer," Diana said.

"No," I said. "I know of Cormac Mac Art because I looked into the background of Cormac McCarthy's name. I'd love to name our dog Cormac, and we could think of him as a king."

"I like Cormac alright, I suppose. You did write the check, after all." Diana turned toward me. "If I help you sell the name to the boys, can we dispense with the hyperbole about ancient Irish kings? It would be such a chore to go through all that when someone asks how he got his name."

"Ah, yes, lassie," I said, "let 'em know 'tis Cormac McCarthy for whom we be namin' the pooch. Aye, and done it is, then."

Several of my customers at Over the Transom have heard me say that Cormac McCarthy's literary crafts-manship is unexcelled, have heard me preach that McCarthy's penchant for infusing violence with a love of language is exquisite. I believe, and have hand-sold the opinion, that Cormac McCarthy's unblinking eye catches man's blood-smeared meanness in the glaring light of his particular art and renders it required viewing. It occurred to me that Mr. McCarthy might not be flattered to share his name with such a sweet, doe-eyed fellow as the Golden Retriever in the backseat of my Jeep. But, if Cormac McCarthy knew that I was a bookseller special-izing in used and rare volumes, that I'd invested $750 for a first edition of *Blood Meridian*, then perhaps he might not judge his name taken in vain.

I shifted my musings to the rumble in my belly, and suggested we stop off at a little café that served blue-plate

lunches, "a meat-and-three place" as Drew called it. I
made up my mind to order the fried chicken and turnip
greens and mashed potatoes and green beans. "Mama
Joe's would be great," Diana agreed, "but what about—"
she paused, "Cormac?"

"I didn't think of that," I said. "Hmm. Well, I don't
want to leave him alone in the Jeep for that long. I guess
we'll just have to skip it and go on home." Printed on the
cover of the folder Mr. Bennett had given me were these
words: *I will take care of you.* And so I would, and it
would mean sacrifice, beginning with the blue-plate special at Mama Joe's. Mr. Bennett had said it might rob my
bank; it would cost money to keep Cormac. And what
had Diana said? *Commitment.* It would take some of that,
too.

"Oh, well," I said. "A homemade peanut-butter and
jelly sandwich doesn't sound so bad."

By the time we pulled into our driveway, both the
boys and the dog were asleep in the backseat. Diana cau-
tiously, quietly opened Dylan's door. I opened the other.
John Luke's eyes popped open right away, as soon as I laid
my hand on his shoulder. He stepped out of the Jeep and
ambled awkwardly toward the house. "What's for lunch?"
John Luke asked and disappeared inside. Dylan slept on
his mother's shoulder. They, too, went inside. I was left
alone with Cormac.

Almost as if he had been waiting for the chance of some privacy, the young Golden opened his eyes but kept his muzzle down on the seat. I bent down, putting my elbows on the car seat, and brought my face close to Cormac's.

"So, want some peanut butter, Cormac?"

Cormac stretched his face toward mine and licked my chin. I closed my eyes and let the pup slobber me down good. "Well, come on, pal. I hope you like crunchy."

FIVE

I SAT ABOARD the swiveling stool behind the sales counter at the bookstore. I kicked the Birkenstock sandal off my right foot and stroked Cormac's head with my toes. He sat on his haunches looking through glass display case at the knees of the man on the other side of the counter.

I had rigged a gate at the open end of the counter to keep Cormac from roaming about the bookstore. Some customers were uncomfortable with him. Most days, I left Cormac at home to play in the yard, to chase any squirrels that dared explore the ground within the fence. He was healthy and active, with a great appetite, and had grown fast. At six months, he now weighed about thirty-five pounds. The first couple of weeks I had to remind the boys not to hand over table scraps, though now and again I did treat Cormac to a teaspoon of peanut butter.

My daughter Emily stopped by the store on her way back to college. She'd come to Fairhope to her mother's place for the weekend. She walked in with a rawhide chew-toy for Cormac. "I can only stay a minute," she said, taking the wrapper off the chew. Cormac knew the treat was for him. His whole being was invested in his eyes and nose as he strained to detect what Emily was about to hand over. "My dog loves these things, too," she said. She told me her young Boxer was in the car, that she'd just got him one of the same chews at the pet supply store. She said she needed to get on the road to Tuscaloosa, gave me a hug and said goodbye, giving a little tug on Cormac's ear. "He's sure good looking," Emily said. With zero modesty I agreed, following her to her car and giving Charlie a pat on the head. Emily said she had tests and a big paper to write and wouldn't be back to Fairhope for three or so weeks. "I'll call when I head back this way," she said. She pulled away from the curb and I saw Drew walking down the sidewalk.

We went inside the bookstore and he came to the counter, leaning forward to get a better look at Cormac. "This mutt's bigger than Zeb, but he's twice as laid back," Drew said. "Some day we'll have to let the two of 'em run, so Cormac can pick up on a little *rambunction*."

"No thanks," I told Drew. "This guy's got the perfect temperament for a used bookstore." Indeed, the space at my feet seemed to suit the young dog, whose curiosity only now and then got him on his feet. I told Drew that Cormac was naturally housetrained. "It's weird," I said. "Even in the backyard he only uses this one small area for his business. And, he's never once peed in the house. I put down newspaper, but he's not interested. Only answers nature's call outside where nature lives. I'm telling you, he's a high-class pup. Most important, he's good company here in the store."

"I bet," Drew replied, a touch of sarcasm easily detectable. "You need some customers in this place, man."

"I'd settle for just one or two to buy a half dozen of my top-shelf books," I answered. "If I sold this one book," I turned on my stool and tapped the spine of the little green octavo volume *Gombo Zhebes*, "I could cover expenses for two months and take home some money, too."

"You gotta be kidding me!" Drew said. "Let me see that book."

"No. Better leave it out of harm's way," I said. "I wouldn't want to take your money if you broke it."

"Oh, bull," Drew said. "I'm not going to break a book."

"So, Zebbie hasn't given you any trouble?"

"Not much. He chased my goats a few times. I wasn't sure what I was going to do to curb the bad habit. Then one of my older billys took care of that." Drew smiled. "I'd headed out to the goat pasture to scold Zebulon when he got a flying lesson from Julius Caesar. He's kept away from the goats ever since."

Drew told me that Zebbie's other infractions were all minor, that he and Linda were glad to have him around.

"And speaking of the little monster, I'd better go. He's in the truck. Plus, I've got a concrete truck due at the job site in ten minutes."

Drew went around to the end of the counter and called Cormac, who jumped up and went to the gate there, standing on his hind legs. Drew petted the red dog. "He is a good-looking retriever."

"Quite the regal beagle, he is," I said. "Plus, he can talk. He's a great conversationalist."

"Like I said, you need some human contact, man. You should start selling beer in this place." Drew headed for the door.

"I'm not kidding," I said, following.

"Oh I believe you," Drew said. "And, like I told *you*, Zeb can fly." He shook his head, then, "What in God's name are you talking about? I'm calling Diana to tell her you're drunk at work."

I laughed and told Drew to come back to the counter with me. I opened the little gate, stepped in and bent over to pat Cormac. His tail whipped from side to side, his eyes lit up. I found his chew-toy, a piece of rawhide twisted on the ends to look like a bone, and offered it to him. Cormac took it, and bobbled his head to adjust the rawhide toward the back of his mouth, holding it crosswise the way he might retrieve a stick.

"Okay, Mick," I said.

"I thought it was Cormac," Drew said.

"It's Cormac. And, Mick or Mickins, depending on the day or my mood," I said. "Sometimes he's just *the doggins*." Doggins was our Tolkien-sounding word for canine friend. Cormac had not waited for me. By the time I returned my attention to him, he was already talking. All he needs to accomplish his special vocalizing is anything at all in his mouth: a leaf the size of a business card, a sock, a baseball cap. The sound he makes is like the moaning of E.T. in the movie before he said, "E.T. phone home." It may not be English, but the guttural, throaty articulation still speaks emotions accurately. There, at the back of Cormac's tongue, over his pink soft palate came sounds best described as like a mother's purring over a sad child, or a grandmother's mewling over her newest grandson.

"You call that *talking*?" Drew asked. "He just wants to bring you something."

"Well," I said, "It is something of a whimper, I admit. But deep and throaty, nonetheless, and endearing. Completely endearing." I challenged him to bring Zebbie to the bookstore for a sound-off contest.

"Zebulon won't concern himself with trivialities like this," Drew said. "His fierce warrior genes compel him to engage in more worthwhile fooling around."

"Like chasing goats?"

"For starters," Drew said. "But the book's not closed yet, pal." Drew punched me on the arm. "I better get going on that one." We walked to the door with Cormac following, talking all the while. He did, in fact, sound sort of silly grunting and moaning around the chew-toy. I leaned down and patted Cormac's head and he immediately assumed the sit position. He tilted his head up, kept talking, kept telling me, no doubt, how much he trusted me to take good care of him.

SIX

"MAYBE I SHOULD'VE brushed you, Cormac." He sat beside me on the passenger seat, perked up, watching the world speed past the window. The clouds hung heavy and low and it looked like it might rain before lunch. "Sostie is coming to see us at the bookstore today."

Betty Fulton, a friend and author from Jackson, Mississippi, was to drop by for a visit this morning as she toured the South for her latest book, *Love and Divorce on the Rocks*. Her husband, my long-time friend, Scott Cannon, and their black and white Collie mix, Sostie, would be coming, too.

Betty had popped in for a visit about three years earlier while in town to do a signing at Page and Palette, another bookstore just up the street. Scott, who loitered in Over the Transom spinning tales of the wealth and power available to us both if we could only get in on the ground floor of the disposable bikini market. When Betty, tall and glamorous, walked in, Scott instantly hit on her. I learned later from Scott, confirmed by Betty,

that he asked her that day if she'd marry him, then the
blessed event took place almost a year later.

"You'll especially like Sostie," I said to Cormac. "She's
such a cutie, and get this, as much a hound for peanut
butter as you," The doggins hiked up his ears and scooted
over on the seat closer to me as if to indicate, "tell me
more."

I took my eyes off the road for a second and lowered
my voice. "My pal Scott did time in Ethiopia in the Peace
Corps. Now listen up, Mick. This gets technical." I thought
about Diana asking if we could skip my discourse on
ancient Irish kings when telling people how Cormac got
his name. "In Amharic, what they speak in Ethiopia," I
said, "the word for three is *sost*. Get my drift?"

Cormac looked at me like I'd grown antlers or something. I took my right hand off the steering wheel and put
it on Cormac's head. "Here," I said, "I'll quote Scott Cannon
himself: 'Sostie is the name for our 3-legged rescue mutt-
puppy because I didn't want Tripod or Lucky or some such
goofy name.'"

I looked over at Cormac. "Oh, I said, she's an older
woman, and very pretty with her three legs. What else do
you need to know?" I'd done my bit at matchmaking, but
his expression asked if there was more to be told. I patted
him, and he accepted that I was finished.

I stopped by Latte Da coffee shop and picked up a

pound of full-city-roast Costa Rican beans for my guests. In my store I ground the coffee beans and got a pot going. Twenty minutes later, Scott and Betty and Sostie walked into the bookstore. Cormac had pranced to Sostie's side before the door even closed. He was bigger than Sostie. They did the requisite sniffing, and some low-key posturing, and then settled down together in the middle of the bookstore floor on a braided oval rug in front of a burnt-sienna couch with lumpy cushions and well-worn arms. I poured the three of us a cup of coffee. Before I sat down I went back to the kitchen and got the peanut butter. I tossed the jar to Scott, along with a spoon.

"You do the honors," I offered. Both dogs were on their feet. Scott spooned out a treat for Sostie and Cormac, right onto the floor.

"On the *carpet*?" Betty said. "Come on, Scott."

"It's okay," I said. "Look at this carpet."

"That's not the point, Sonny," said Betty. "I'm still trying to train the dog." She pointed to Scott. "*Him.*"

"Oh, just you watch," Scott said. "Two tiny wet spots that will be dried and disappear within a week."

Cormac finished his peanut butter and came to lie at my feet. Sostie jumped on the sofa between Betty and Scott. Scott asked about Cormac, said his face and demeanor reminded him of the Yellow Labrador who had stayed by his father's side for fifteen years. I told him about Zebbie, about Drew adopting him, and about our finding Cormac some seven months ago. "He'll be a year old March 21," I told Scott and Betty.

"He's going to be a big fellow," Scott said.

"I think so. Maybe seventy-five pounds when he's fully grown," I said.

Betty stayed quiet. "So, Betty, how's the new novel going?" I asked.

"Three weeks on the top ten best-seller list," she said, offhandedly, as though the information were not important. "Look, Sonny, what about you? On this tour, I've heard of three independent bookstores closing. I'm talking about shops that have name recognition. T-shirt worthy. I want to know what's going on with your store."

"Well, I think I'm going to have to close Over the Transom," I said, the words tumbling out. I couldn't believe I'd just spoken aloud the thing that I'd been thinking in a dusty, cobwebbed corner of my mind for some weeks now. Saying it was like making real what had been before only a possibility. I was disconcerted as though I just got the news myself.

"You have to fight for it," Scott said flatly. He got up and walked over to a bin of T-shirts. Sostie followed. So did Cormac. They sat and gazed up at Scott as he took a shirt and held it out in front of himself so he could read it aloud:

There is nothing so important as the book can be.
–*MAXWELL PERKINS*
[Because] All that man has done, gained, or been: it is
lying as in magic preservation in the pages of books.
–*THOMAS CARLYLE*

Scott checked the size, declared it a fit. "Do you mean what you've got written here?"

"You know I do," I said.

Scott draped the T-shirt over the crook of his arm while he pulled off his own white oxford and dropped it on the floor. Bare-chested, he pushed out his chest and curled his arms into a muscle-man pose, then pulled the T-shirt over his head.

Betty looked at me. "You want him back?" Scott and I had once been partners in a small publishing concern. Cormac, in the meantime, had grabbed the shirt on the floor and made off with it, dragging it to his spot behind the counter. Sostie trailed him, hopping along on her one front leg. Scott went after them, patting Betty's shoulder as he went past.

"Haven't you got something you could sell?" Betty asked.

"Everything I've got is mortgaged for more than it's worth." I told Betty and Scott that I thought I should schedule an appointment with a bankruptcy lawyer. "Just to discuss my options, you know."

"Oh, my God!" Betty said. "You can't be serious."

"Completely, I'm afraid." I told them the money I had in my store checking account could cover overhead for two more months.

"Does Diana know this?"

I told Betty she knew about the store's cash flow drying up. "But we didn't talk about meeting with a lawyer."

"Good," Betty said. "We've got to talk some sense into you." She got up and paced back and forth. She stopped and faced me. "What about the novel you've been working on? Why don't you sell that?" Her question surprised me.

"I don't think anybody would buy that book," I said. "And I still lack a hundred pages or so to finish it.

"How do you know no one will buy it?" she replied. "I sold my last three books on proposal. If you've got a good start, and they like it, they'll offer you a contract to complete it."

"What have you got to lose?" Scott chimed in.

"I will use my considerable influence in New York to get the manuscript read," she offered, completely serious.

Cormac pranced and capered, following Scott back to the middle of the room. Sostie came along as well. Scott said, "Betty can get this done. Her agent will read it right away and tell us what she thinks."

Cormac stood, put his muzzle on my thigh, and rolled his eyes upward at me. He did this more and more these days, and each time he parked his face there the world seemed a little less with me. This must be the part of being near a dog that's been shown to lower old people's blood pressure in assisted living places and such. I reached out my hand and rubbed his head. He wagged his tail. "Cormac thinks it's a good idea," I said, smiling.

"What more validation do you want?" Betty asked.

"It's a long shot, you have to admit," I said, wanting to bring some reality to the fantastical notion that a publisher would buy my book.

"Sure it is," Betty said. "But you miss a hundred percent of the shots you don't take."

"It beats sitting for the life insurance underwriter's exam," Scott said. I agreed and said I'd think about it. They said they had to get rolling to Tallahassee. As I walked them to the door, I wondered how Cormac would behave as Sostie left the building. Had she smitten this young dog with her beauty? It seemed no. Cormac only walked as far as the front door. At the threshold he turned and went back to his place behind the counter, curling down for a nap.

I stepped onto the sidewalk to watch my friends walk away and felt the first drops of rain. Several parking spaces on the street were empty and I saw no pedestrians.

This damp, gray day could be well-spent at home relaxed in my leather chair, my sock feet propped on the hassock. Since I was fantasizing, I took it further, imagined my laptop on my knees, coffee on a tray table beside me as I worked on the great American novel. It was not a picture I could bring into clear focus.

I went back inside. It was 10:30. An hour and a half into a business day without a customer. I went to my stool behind the counter and woke up the Toshiba's screen: one internet order for a $35 used book, *Lanterns on the Levee: Recollections of a Planter's Son* by William Alexander Percy, a good 1941 hardcover 4th printing with a clean dustjacket. I looked at Cormac, asleep on a small rug. The hair on his shoulders was a little darker red than the rest and getting curly. He was a handsome, laid-back doggins.

"You make it look so easy, Mick."

He didn't even blink. "If I get a book published, pal," I said, "I'll sure thank you for your part." I went to find the Percy book, wondering at the little hope stirring in my head, hope that I'd have to make good on my promise to Cormac.

I walked, pacing slowly between rows of shelves sagging only just perceptibly with their quiet books. Cormac was at my heels, his pink tongue hanging from the side of his mouth, his eyes bright with expectation that we were going on some adventure, tail swishing.

I walked back to the counter, then behind it. Cormac stopped on the customer side and stared at me. His tail stopped. He pulled his tongue into his mouth and cocked his head. His eyes signaled confusion, as if, "Okay, so what are we looking for?" He sat, continued to look at me. I looked at him.

"I'm thinking about something."

For about the fifth time that day, as the day passed, I strolled the floor of my empty bookstore.

"That's it," I said. "I've made up my mind."

I looked at the big grandfather clock in the corner near the front door. "It's five o'clock and time to go home, boy." I snapped the leash to Cormac's collar before stepping onto the sidewalk. I still couldn't trust that he wouldn't dash in front of a car coming down the street. He was a good heeler ninety percent of the time; the other ten percent he'd sprint without warning and ignore all commands, even the call of his name. These times a dog or cat or a person had one hundred percent of his attention. Until we got that behavior modified, the leash was the only safe option for going from the bookstore to the Jeep. I let Cormac jump into the passenger's seat, rolled down his window halfway, and closed his door. I went around and slid behind the wheel.

"Well, today we walked several hundred miles in a

bookstore," I told Cormac. "But it paid off." I looked over at him. He was on full alert, his ears perked up as he watched a cat ease out from between some bushes and onto the sidewalk. "I made up my mind to send out the manuscript myself," I said. Cormac put his head out the window and barked. His tail swatted me on the face. I read somewhere that cats sleep about sixteen hours a day, two-thirds of their lives. This big red dog of mine, I believed, would spend about half his life wagging his tail. If Cormac wore T-shirts, I think his favorite would read: Wag more, bark less.

SEVEN

"YOU KNOW HOW I feel about your writing," Diana said,
rinsing her hands in the kitchen sink. "I've told you for a
year that you should send out your novel. You know how
to write," she told me, "and you're writing a good book."
She asked me what had broken the inertia. I told her the
plan was mostly Cormac's doing, and slipped a little grin.

"So, does Cormac also have a plan for submitting
your unfinished novel to an editor?" she asked. "You
don't know how to make a publishing deal." I told her I'd
just take it one step at a time, maybe start with an editor
I'd met the previous October at the Southern Book Festival in Nashville.

"She invited me at the time I met her to send my
book," I said.

"Why don't you include a photo of Cormac, and a
cover letter from him as your agent?"

Diana joined me at the kitchen table. Cormac, on
hearing his name spoken, came over and put his chin on
my knee. "Probably not a bad idea," I said, and rubbing

his head. I told Diana I'd just read that a photo of a Golden Retriever was almost as effective at demanding attention in advertising as a scantily clad woman.

"Maybe so," she said, pointing out that the real estate sign on the house for sale just down the street bore a Golden Retriever's face. "Should I take the photo then?" Diana asked, teasing. "Or will you?"

The next morning I decided to walk to the bookstore. In the night the late September wind had shifted around to the north and the air was clean and crisp, and the sun had a cloudless blue sky all to itself. The incomplete manuscript of my novel was in a manila envelope under my arm. Cormac was smart, easy on the leash, only now and again muscling away from me and drawing his collar against his neck so that he coughed. I'd give the leash a little snap, then tell him sternly, *heel*, and he'd stop pulling.

He was putting on weight: sixty-three pounds last vet check and growing quickly. But he wasn't fat. With our daily walks, he would stay in good shape.

By the time we'd covered half the distance to the store, I had made up my mind to call an old friend in San Francisco. He had once told me that when I was ready to submit my novel, he knew an agent who'd help me put it into the right hands. When I had opened the store, I called him, told him the big day had arrived. He said he'd call the agent right away, and ask her to phone me herself.

She phoned within the half hour, introduced herself as Amy Rennert. She said, "So you've got a book I should look at?" Easy as that, this thing was rolling. She invited me to email the first thirty pages to her, and she'd get back to me. She phoned back the same day and offered to represent me. She said she believed we could sell my unfinished book.

Cormac looked at the package I'd tossed onto the floor. Who needed hard copy in a quick-transference world? He sat on his woven rug, mostly looking out the window, his nose to the daylight outside. But when he'd turn his head back inside the store, he'd look again down at the manila envelope on the floor.

"It's my book," I told him. "What do you think of the first two hundred pages of *The Poet of Tolstoy Park*?" His interest was elsewhere. He just looked at the envelope, then rolled his big eyes at me, without even sniffing in its direction. I moved from the counter and sat in my favorite overstuffed chair, a funky green wingback near the front window with plenty of light streaming in. I called Cormac over. Area rugs were scattered all around the store, and close by was a favorite oval number. He lay down immediately, as if he knew we were in for the long haul.

I really don't know why, but something about the big reddish brown dog stretched out on the braided rug in the middle of the bookstore made me think of a Kerouac poem. A couple of lines from *The Scripture of the Golden Eternity*: "Everything's alright, we're not here, there, or anywhere./ Everything's alright, cats sleep."

And in the midst of my little turmoil, my dog asleep. I studied him lying there. In this very present moment, and in every moment we shared, I could count on his empathy. His sweet brown eyes said he'd fix it all for me, always.

Within the week, Amy called to say a publisher was going to make an offer. Two days later, I talked to Drew, told him I thought we were close to making a deal on the book. I told him I'd not heard back from my agent, but I didn't want to jinx the deal by seeming impatient.

"*Seeming* impatient? Man, you are impatient," Drew said. "With good cause, son. Take a man pill and call your agent," I told him I would do that before going home from the store that day. I waited until I had locked the door of the bookstore to call Amy. I was behind the wheel of my Jeep, Cormac on the seat beside me. I was nervous and could hardly aim my fingers at the keys on the cell phone.

"I was just about to phone you," Amy said, and I swear I heard a note of defeat in her voice. But before I could further catastrophize the moment, Amy said, "Here's what I got you." She went down the list of deal points.

I sat there in broad daylight with tears in my eyes. I blinked and looked over at Cormac. He had curled down on the seat. His eyes were closed. Then my agent tested the strength of my man pill.

"That's the good news," Amy said.

Everyone knows the phrase that follows: *And now for the bad news.*

What in the sweet name of Jesus could that be? In the nanosecond pause, my mind scrolled through a half dozen devastating possibilities. "This is October," Amy said, "and they want the book by May 1. Can you write the rest of the book sustaining what you've got going in those first two hundred pages?" She reminded me that I had a wife and children and Thanksgiving and Christmas and et cetera to consider. "Not to mention a bookstore," she added. She told me we'd be signing a contract and that it would not be a good thing to miss my first deadline. I interrupted her. "Just tell me where to sign."

Yes, yes, yes.

I put my hand wide-fingered on the head of my Mickins. He opened his eyes and cut them over at me. He knew something was up. He got up on the seat and stared at me, his ears alert. He pushed his face near my own. He licked my cheek, pulled back to see if that helped. I grinned like Alice's cat and his tail thumped the door panel.

EIGHT

IT WAS CLEAR that I'd have to stay home to write to meet the deadline for *The Poet of Tolstoy Park*. I had to figure out what to do about keeping the bookstore open for walk-ins.

Cormac and I went to Pierre's baseball card and vintage LP record store to ask for advice. I found him putting away a stack of albums. "Check this out," he said. "The Beatles' *White Album* on the Apple label, 1968. It's an original copy, with the poster and four photos. Picked it up at the thrift store for a quarter. I might get fifty bucks for it." I told him that was a good margin of return.

"So what's up?" Pierre asked. He patted Cormac on the head, who stayed at his knee only for a moment. He headed off to check out the rest of the record store. "What brings you to my little corner of world trade?"

I told him I had to figure out how to keep my store open while I knuckled down at home to finish the novel and a rewrite before May. "No problem," he said, still shuffling records, like this was the easiest thing in the world. "I'll move into your store and take care of every-thing." He told me he'd already been thinking about it. Word had quickly traveled around town about my book deal.

"What do you mean, you'll move in?" I asked.

"Just that," he said. "My lease expired here a month ago, and I'm on a month-to-month basis with my land-lord. I've been looking for a different storefront." Pierre told me he'd move his inventory onto the premises at Over the Transom. "The floor space is big enough, easily," Pierre said, adding he would sell my books for me in exchange for free rent and use of the phone and fax machine and computer. "I know your books as well as you."

I didn't hesitate. "When can you make the move?"

"This afternoon," he said, then added that he could get some high school students to help him start the move tomorrow, and get it done by the weekend. "I can be in business at your place next week."

"Pierre, this is great. It works for us both," I said.

"You just set your mind on finishing that book," he said. "This is your chance. Don't blow it."

"Oh, I believe I can do it," I said. "And, all the better with your help. I'm grateful, Pierre. I don't know what I would have done."

"God, stop fawning," Pierre said. "Just be sure I get a part in the movie. Will there be a mud wrestling scene?"

I told him that would be small payment, and I'd write the scene with him in mind. And with a handshake for good measure and to seal the deal, I called Cormac and we headed back to the bookstore. Cormac walked with his head high and his tail sweeping side to side. With a spunky air to his carriage and a spring in my own step, I wasn't sure either of us could even finish out a week behind the counter.

Diana agreed this was a good plan. She and the boys and I celebrated that night with supper at Benny's Pizza Shop. It took some talking to get John Luke and Dylan to understand why with me at home each day they couldn't give up going to school. They became more agreeable when I promised to pick them up early on some days and join them at school for lunch now and again.

"You can go on my field trips," said John Luke.

"Will you bring the cookies to the birthday parties?" Dylan asked.

"Yep," I said to them both. I'll even try my hand at writing a novel, I thought.

The morning of our first day into the new routine, Cormac waited for me at the door, ready to go to the bookstore. "Not today, Mickins," I said. I went back to the kitchen for another cup of coffee, instead of out the door to the Jeep and town. Cormac stood in the foyer tossing looks at me over his shoulder. He turned to stare at the door, his pose reminding me of the hunting dog he really was. He could have been waiting among the cattails on the shore of an icy lake, ready to jump in to retrieve some duck I'd just shot. But I'm not a shooter, and he's not a retriever of more than the occasional tennis ball or Frisbee.

He could, however, now be something of a farm dog, romping and playing all day instead of hanging out with me inside a bookstore. He could chase squirrels, bother the cat, and cut up with the next-door dog, Bailey, also a Golden Retriever but almost completely white. Our two-acre place was only six minutes out of town proper and still within the city limits, but with not many houses, almost no streetlights, it felt like another world. Cormac, like Hank the Cow Dog of the children's books, was placed in charge of "ranch" security.

In his new role, the tiny part of our backyard that had been enclosed by the fence seemed unfair limitation on such important responsibility. I'd take down the chain-link fence that Diana never liked anyway because it was "so ugly" and have an electronic fence installed. With me working at my desk in the study, the Mick could rule the world of squirrels and birds. And with the new fence buzzing away, I'd not worry that he'd wander off.

The man on the phone told me the "fence" would amount to a thin wire buried a few inches deep in the soil. The wire was not expensive, so I'd have the entire two acres circumscribed. With the two ends of the wire connected to a transmitter, and a collar that had a built-in receiver to pick up the wire's frequency pulse, Cormac would get a mild shock if he tried to cross where the wire was buried. But not before sounding a warning beep so that Cormac could engage his superior intelligence and stay away from the ouch place.

Until then, he was certain that he was supposed to be inside with me. And not only with me inside the house, but that he should take every step I took. Almost literally. If I got up from my desk to get another cup of coffee, he came along. If I walked to a window to enjoy the view of the big dogwood tree just down the hill, he'd have his own look-see.

Three years later, Cormac still does this, follows me all over the house, though I think his clinging to me nowadays is in large measure a consequence of his nightmarish adventure, like the way he sinks flat on the floor when I start packing for travel. Sometimes when I move from room to room, I speed up to get ahead of him and then duck behind a door to jump out as he passes and scare him the way Dylan likes to do to me. Cormac has not yet once appeared even remotely startled by my antics. I'm pretty sure it's his nose that lets him see around corners. When I leap out with a big *yaah*! he only looks at me with his big brown eyes worried that I've lost it.

My new life as a novelist was like a monk's insight after a long trek toward some evasive truth. Those first weeks of long hours spent writing, there was a time or two when I wanted to pinch myself: Emmylou Harris singing from the stereo, sweat pants and bare feet all day, my protagonist's story unfolding for me like I had it all on tape, my dog on the floor while I pecked away at the computer keyboard. We had it easy. If I turned my head in his direction, he'd watch my eyes to see if I needed him to fetch something. But I did all the work and just let Cormac guard the muse so he wouldn't abandon us. Cormac did a good job.

In the space of about a month my whole life had turned around, the cavalry had come riding over the hill, publishing contract in velvet-gloved hand. Sonny the novelist. I had the papers to prove it. Diana told me she'd known it all along, and had many times tried to tell me so. She reminded me more than once that Thoreau said our focus determines our reality. "Seems I remember," Diana said, "saying something like you should focus on your writing." She had told me precisely that.

And Cormac. Bless him. The doggie would not have to fret that any day might find me poking around in a bare cupboard, looking for a bone, and the poor dog would have none. *No, sir.* Cormac was ruler of his two acres. Until, that is, the king would one day feel abandoned upon his lands, and then a keen, deep fretting would extend the edges of his world into the outer dark.

NINE

Two thick-armed men in tight T-shirts pulled into my driveway with an array of supplies and wire-burying tools. Neither would step out of the pickup when the big reddish-brown dog bounded up to greet them. My friendly Cormac, a tail-swishing 75-pounder, standing down a 400-pound pair of men.

"Cormac! Leave the fellows alone. They don't love you the way I do," I said. My voice wasn't loud enough to be heard over the rumble coming from the hole in the truck's muffler. Neither did my smile get to them. They were stone-faced, frowning, and not about to step out of their truck until I did something with Cormac. The driver switched off the engine.

"Don't worry, men," I told them.

They didn't budge.

"I'll take him inside the house," I offered.

"You want this wire buried in the dirt, you'll do that," the driver said. It seemed odd to me that these men who installed underground dog fences would be afraid of dogs. But I guess it wasn't in their job description to deal with dogs, only to bury wire.

Cormac headed for the front door, every few steps looking over his shoulder toward the men still in the truck. I let him cross the threshold then closed the door. I walked back outside to discuss the work with the guys, each now taking a small machine trencher from the bed of the truck. I turned back to look at the house. Cormac had gone into my son's bedroom and straight to the window there. He found the blinds raised and the curtains drawn back. He took his post, and fixed us in his stare the way a bank security guard watches a man with sunglasses and a ball cap third in line for the teller window.

I introduced myself. The driver, John, was the leader. I shook hands with both men, and showed them the layout of my two acres, told them I wanted to be sure the wire was set deeply enough that it didn't migrate upward into the blade of my lawn mower. "We know 'bout that," said John.

"Yes," I said. "I imagine you do." I told them I was grateful they'd responded so quickly to my call. Again John spoke. "We go where we sent. And we ain't gettin' nothin' done talkin'." Without so much as a word passing between them, the two men fell in tandem to their work, each starting the engine on his trencher and tilting the spinning blade into the soil of my yard. Dirt spewed as they cut the narrow slit, going off in opposite directions from a single starting point. Their work was precise, their movements fluid and graceful, and they spoke not a word.

They'd not covered twenty yards each when Cormac came out the garage doors. I'd forgot the downstairs door was open into the garage, and the garage doors were open. This time the canine confrontation went differently—for two reasons, I think:

First: The men were working.

When a man gets going with his work, gets in the groove, not much can keep him from his appointed rounds. The task is not about excavating a trench of a certain length. It's about putting one foot in front of the other, hands sure and deft on the machine, and then a ditch happens.

This time Cormac did not faze these men. Maybe not even lightning splitting the heavens would have disturbed their trenching. I once watched a man dig a ditch in the rain of a thunderstorm and every time the sky burst with lightning and thunder shook the trees, he sped up. A trenching machine could not have dug a hundred feet any faster.

Second: Cormac looked goofy and sounded silly with my son's football jammed crossways in his mouth, open so wide it looked as though his jaw had come loose at the hinge. His eyes bulged and he was trying to talk around the football. Drew would love to see this, I thought.

The men were now compelled to look at the dog standing a few feet away from them. They let their machines come to a quiet idle. Cormac stopped still, not approaching them any closer, as if respectful of their work. This time the mens' eyes conveyed not caution or fear, but a kind of incredulity at the mumbling dog.

Cormac's articulations, shall we say, have two distinctly different voices. The first one he accomplishes with something in his mouth. Cormac's second voice is a kind of purr he uses when he's really laid back, like just waking up in the morning, a language I think he learned from our cat, Smokey. He will sit and look up at me as I'm putting on my socks, and with each exhale he goes, "awwwrrrrhhh." Of course, I echo his sound, but only when we've got the room to ourselves. Our family hasn't yet witnessed or overheard our unusual dialogue.

The men surveyed the spectacle before them, looked at each other, and both grinned and shook their heads. Cormac's football and humming had completely hooked them. The bigger man, John's helper, laughed aloud. "Look there," he said. "Ain't that dog a sight?"

"Cormac, put down the football! That's not yours," I said. He dropped his head, got a case of sad eyes, but kept his clamp on the pigskin. "Dylan's gonna tie your ears together." I put my fists on my hips and cooked up my best fake scowl. "Cormac!"

"Hey, man. Why you wanna call a good dog like him somethin' nasty like Floormat?" John rested, using his trencher handle like a walking cane. He caught his breath behind a laugh. Still flashing a good smile he said, "You oughta call him King, or somethin'. Floormat ain't a name for a dog."

"No," I said, catching the smile. "Not *floormat*. His name is Cormac. C-O-R-M-A-C."

And Cormac sounds phonetically close to cognac. When I would later be on the trail of my lost dog, and a veterinary assistant would tell me they'd had a Golden Retriever in their clinic whose name was *Cognac*, I believed that whoever had brought him there had read the name Cormac off his tag. I knew also my name and contact information on the same tag had been ignored.

"*Cormac,* you say?" John asked. "What kinda name is that?"

"The name of a king in old Ireland," I answered.

"Why don't you jus' call him King? Be easier, wouldn't it?"

"I expect it would," I said. I thought of Diana's entreaty to drop the talk of Irish kings. It seemed unavoidable. "But he likes his name. You hear him talking, don't you? He told me himself he likes to be called

Cormac." I could not have known this talking thing I kidded about would one day help me ID him, and help the negotiations to get him home.

John just shook his head. "Come on, man," he said to his partner. "We don't get to diggin' my truck payment be callin' me Nate the Late."

The wire was laid in less than two hours. I thanked the men, who told me the trainer would be along soon after they left. "We supposed to call quick as we hit the driveway. He be right along with the bill." John bent to rub Cormac's head. "You just take good care of old King here," he said. "He a good dog."

I called Cormac away from his inspection of the newly turned earth lining the edge of our yard. I lay down on the warm grass. Closed my eyes against the morning sun. Cormac came to stand right above me. He stood still, his handsome head poised above me. He looked down at me for a long minute. Then he shook his head, his ears and lips flapping, and walked away like he had business and couldn't lollygag around with me. Already taking over security. I was so proud of him.

Turns out, he was on his way to say good morning to Bailey, the neighbor Golden. I like to think our neighbor Janet so loved our Cormac that when her Cocker Spaniel died of old age, her first thought for a new pet was a Golden.

The trainer soon showed up and went right to work putting little white flags into the ground every few feet along the trench around the entire perimeter of our property. He installed the transmitter on the wall of the barn. I was beginning to think I'd have to learn on my own how to train Cormac, when he came walking toward me with a green collar that had a receiver attached to it about the size of a box of matches.

"My name's Ken," he said. "You'll want to listen up here while I tell you how to do this." He instructed me matter-of-factly to walk my dog along the flagged perimeter, but away from the shock zone that extended five feet on either side of the wire. "A smart dog," Ken said, "is gonna *get it* with only two, not more than three 'corrections.' He'll hear that little beep and bounce away." Ken grinned for the first time.

"And what about our morning walks down Moseley Road?" I asked. "Do I take off his collar and lead him across the wire buried under the driveway?"

"Oh, no. You can't do that," Ken said abruptly. "That would just confuse him. You'll have to load him into your car without the collar and haul him to the end of the drive. That way he thinks the only way across is in a vehicle." It sounded bothersome, but it made sense. That's the way we'd do it.

Ken had me snap a leash on Cormac and walk him

near the flags but outside the shock zone, now activated. He told me to walk the entire line slowly. "Should I let him get a correction?" I asked, frowning.

"No. You never lead him into the shock zone," Ken said. "Never call him into the shock zone."

"I'd never do that," I said.

"Some people are stupid," Ken said, looking away. He told me to take the leash off Cormac. "The dog's curious. He'll check it out, and learn his first lesson. It'll take more than once, probably."

Cormac, brilliant animal that he is, got it with one zap. Afterwards, he refused to go within twenty-five feet of those angry white flags, though he could not figure out why Bailey could wander around the flags with impunity.

TEN

IT WAS A TWENTY-MINUTE walk from my house to the round house where the idea for my new book was conceived. I put my laptop in the leather and canvas bag, slung the strap over my shoulder, and took my cap from one of the pegs on the old hat rack near the front door. From one of its hooks, I took down Cormac's leash.

I glimpsed my image in the hall mirror. Odd, I thought, I don't look like a man who is almost finished with a novel. I looked the same as I did yesterday. I had believed for decades that book writers breathe rarefied air so laced with the bearded sorcerer's most powerful and sparkliest dust that they become transubstantiated into different beings. I really thought sometimes I had opened a bookstore for proximity to the magic. But the mirror revealed no change. At least I had not gone invisible there like a vampire. These last four months, I'd been so totally absorbed in writing the book that on some days I'd behaved like a creature in a scary movie.

Like yesterday.

Diana had walked into my study. I didn't acknowledge she was there because I was struggling at that
moment to fix a transition in the story. Every sentence I
wrote was clunky and awkward. "Still working on the
ending?" she asked. I looked at the clock on the wall
opposite my desk.

"Try an hour on the same paragraph," I said, my eyes
on the words on the screen. I kept my fingers on the keyboard, and didn't look at Diana, hoping she'd cut short
her visit.

"Sometimes," she said, "when you get stuck it's best
to walk away and come back with fresh eyes." She had
stepped over beside me, laying her hand on my shoulder.
"Maybe you'd like to put down the writing for an evening
of dinner and a movie with the boys and me."

I shrugged my shoulder as if to dislodge her hand.

"You know," Diana said, moving to the corner of my
desk. I looked up at her. "We've given you about all the
space you could ask for since before Thanksgiving. You've
hardly joined us at all for anything away from the house.
One night wouldn't—"

"I've got to get this problem worked out now," I said.
"If I take an interruption, I might lose the little bit of
progress I've made."

"An interruption?" Diana asked, her voice tight. "You
could call it a break. You could call it family time." She left

me alone in my study. By the time I'd stopped sulking and was ready to apologize, to ask what movies were playing, all the voices in the house had become silent behind the shutting of the front door. I sat for a moment longer, and then noticed Cormac was not in the room with me. I went out front and called him.

It was dusk, and I waited for him to stroll into the faint light spreading onto the porch and into the yard. I didn't see him, didn't hear the jingle of tags on his collar. I called him again, louder. Still no Cormac. I felt a nudge of panic. Three days ago, I'd left him outside in the afternoon, and he'd run across the wire to go exploring. I was buried in the book, and hadn't even thought of him until I got a call from a neighbor that Cormac was at their house. Now I'd let him run off again. I yelled his name and headed down the steps. He came running full tilt around the corner.

"You scared me," I said. His look said he had wondered when I'd miss him. *Priorities* was a word spoken in my head. Cormac sat, his tail still, and stared up at me. I made a mental note to call the people who sold me the underground fence again. I'd phoned once to complain Cormac was charging out of the yard.

"There's a better transmitter and receiver," Ken had said. We agreed on another two hundred and fifty bucks for a system upgrade. "I guarantee no dog, and only a few elephants will cross this baby," he had said, his attempt at comedy. But I had not yet heard back from Ken.

Cormac and I were both oblivious just now to transmitters and receivers. We were headed for a walk. I had his leash in my hand and he was jumping like a mullet on a run. Every time I got his leash and for one reason or another delayed snapping it to his collar, he'd do a kind of bouncing levitation act. I swear I can't see how he's bending his legs and bunching his muscles when he does this. He gets happy for a walk and springs into the air, his body still mostly horizontal, grinning, his big tongue flopping out of his mouth. On the fourth or fifth airborne maneuver you want to say, "Jeez! It's just a walk, just like the last one we took, just like the next one we'll take." But what you really want is to find a way in your complicated human mind to let go and get some of his simple, saturated joy for yourself.

I had to wait for him to come in for a landing to clip on his leash.

"Come on, Mick, let's go put a bow on this package," I said. I wanted to work on the book's last pages at the round house of Henry Stuart. I first saw it twenty-five years ago, a strange-looking circular hut with a domed roof made of hand-poured concrete blocks. It sat in the middle of a paved parking lot situated between two rows of office buildings. Shaded by a single huge live oak with thick branches that dangled with Spanish moss, the hermit hut, as some know it, looked transported from a movie set, or a Hobbit shire.

In 1982 I became divorced and I was free to make some changes in my life. I went looking for a job that gave me more free time to write during the day. First, to help clear my head of emotional baggage, I spent six months of muscle-wringing work, barebacked under a hot sun tending the decks of barges shoved by a tugboat up and down the Tennessee Tombigbee Waterway.

Then I thought about moving to New York or Los Angeles, but my daughter, Emily, was living near Fairhope, and I wouldn't miss my weekend visits with her. So, if not a writerly loft in Manhattan, then a garage apartment in Fairhope and real estate sales seemed a good next option. Opening a bookstore, at this point, was not even a twinkle in my eye.

When I'd shown up for my first real estate class at an office complex just north of Fairhope, I was surprised to find the odd little round house squarely in the middle of the parking lot. It looked dropped there from some ancient time, seeming all the more out of place with asphalt crowding it on three sides. When I asked, a woman told me I was looking at "some kind of a house" built in the 1920s by an eccentric old man. The life story of that man, Henry James Stuart, would come to inform a book I'd write twenty-some years later.

When Cormac and I took our little hikes, I could hear Henry's voice better, his story became more accessible. Strolling with Cormac I was more receptive to Henry Stuart's ghost floating above the land. So a regular part of our schedule was long walks with Cormac to keep my mind open to the character. Two-thirds of *The Poet of Tolstoy Park* was stirred loose in my imagination by those walks. The best advice for writer's block, for me: "Go walk the dog." I knew I'd write imperfect fiction. But God didn't stop with a few fine examples of pine trees, and I had decided to raise up my own tree in the forest.

We went outside on the porch to greet the April morning's warmth, and struck out for the round house. I led Cormac to the Jeep to load him up for his short ride down the driveway, across the shock zone. "You know," I said to him. "This is a pain in the neck. I wonder if— hmmm?" It suddenly seemed to me that a vehicle is a vehicle and a child's red wagon qualifies as a vehicle for transporting a dog down a driveway. "Let's try this," I said. Cormac seemed game.

I went to the garage and got the boys' wagon. The wooden side rails seemed perfect, would give the doggins a more secure ride. I pulled the wagon by its handle onto the driveway, and called for Cormac to get aboard. I bent over at the front, snapped my fingers inside the wagon.

He started to get excited, picked up a piece of pine straw and vocalized his enthusiasm and curiosity and confusion. His tail swung back and forth with such energy that it would have raised a welt if it had struck a leg. Then it dawned on me. When loading him in the Jeep, I always said the same thing to him: "Get in the Jeep."

So I snapped my fingers over the wagon and said, "Cormac, get in the Jeep." He jumped right in, and took a seat, his tail hanging off the back of the wagon like a rudder moving side to side. We must have looked perfectly ridiculous. The drivers in both cars that passed as we rolled down the driveway broke into wide grins when they saw us, a man tugging a wagon load of reddish-brown dog. I didn't care. And we crossed the fence that way each morning that we walked until we moved to another house years later.

Once at the street, I called Cormac from the wagon and we continued our hike to the round house. We dawdled, stopping two or three times for Cormac to sniff out some mysterious passage written on a bush or in the grass, which he occasionally snacked on after a brief reading.

"There have been some passages by McCarthy or Marquez that have made me feel the same way, Mickins," I said at one such stop. I could have added other names of other writers who wrote stuff good enough to chow down on, but I don't think Cormac would have recognized them. Ah, so much good writing, so little time. The great writers I love to read were an influence on my writing, but they also kept me from trying my own hand at fiction. Gabriel García Márquez, William Faulkner, Cormac McCarthy. I stood in stunned awe of their work. What was the point? If I couldn't write that well, why spend the ink?

When we got to the round house, Cormac yipped and wiggled. He looked at the door, then back at me, then back at the door. I thought there might be some animal inside, a mouse, a stray cat. I thought of a snake, like the one I'd written into a scene in the book. I opened the narrow double-doors slowly, Cormac nudging at my calves. There were no visitors inside. At least that I could see. As my dog pushed past me into the circular room I wondered, for the twenty-third time, if Henry might be on the premises, and Cormac knew it. He looked around, sniffed the chair I always chose at the table, then struck his lizard-on-a-rock pose, stretching out flat as a rug on the floor. Before I could get my laptop out of the bag and powered-up, the novel file opened, Cormac's eyes were closed. He'd made himself at home in Henry's place.

Somehow in that mysterious place Henry seemed nearer. He'd called his land Tolstoy Park, and I talked myself into believing I could also feel Tolstoy there in the background.

I sat down at a table near a window. I slipped off my shoes and stretched my toes over to scratch Cormac's back. He immediately rolled onto his side and kicked his legs up. He wanted a belly rub. Somebody once told me that a dog turns over onto its back to indicate submission. And if they're signaling a human, they will either curl their tail to cover their privates, or, if they trust you they won't bother to cover up. Cormac's tail was relaxed. He hadn't given up on me.

I opened my notes file, scrolled down to find the list of people whose names I'd put into the acknowledgements section at the front of the book. I enjoyed constructing a brief narrative that told of each person's help to me as I wrote *The Poet of Tolstoy Park*. When I finished, I'd added a page and a half to my manuscript. I was about to save and close the file, when Cormac gave a big sigh and turned over on his side, so completely at rest that I thought about joining him on the cool, shiny concrete floor of the round house. I watched his chest and belly rise and fall, watched his eyebrows twitch following the dream show in his head, and put my fingers back on the keyboard and wrote:

"And good old Cormac, my dog, lay so patiently near me as I wrote the book reminding me, like Kerouac's cat, there is, finally, nothing so great about human endeavor or failings that should disturb our rest."

It is interesting to me, this touch of irony: that Cormac himself inspired the counter maxim to his paragraph in my book's acknowledgements. For when I lost my good dog Cormac, oh, how that failing disturbed my rest, and, curiously enough while walking in the bookwriter's shoes.

ELEVEN

First, the loud *whump* startled me. Second, it surprised me to discover its source.

The house was empty except for me. Diana had gone to work, and the boys were off to school. I hadn't noticed the gathering dark in the clouds to the west. There was a low sonorous roll of distant thunder. I went to the front door and stepped out onto the porch. The wind rose, whipping the tall pines in my front yard.

There was the sound again. A thud, like something striking a wall. It was coming from inside. I went back into the house. The big thump came again. I went down the hall, into the kitchen. Then I saw Cormac, outside on the back porch, heaving himself against the French door. He stood on his hind legs to reach as high as he possibly could. I let him inside and, whining, he went around and around my legs. I sat down at the dining room table and patted my knees. Cormac came to lie on the floor, looking at me with his face between his paws. When the thunder boomed again, he jumped up and looked over his shoulder, then sat on his haunches between my knees. I looked at him, then sat on the floor and petted him, rubbing his head and down his back, until his breathing slowed to a normal rhythm.

I could not imagine what had changed for the doggins. Last week he had paid no mind to rumbling in the heavens; today the sound of thunder terrified him. It would come to pass that even the sound of rain would give him the jitters—Pavlov's bell and all that. Cormac had, on some esoteric cue, reached back into his canine ancestry, back to a cave and the sound of a giant boulder rolling down a hill, to one of his forefathers smushed by the big rock, broken like the skull of a saber-tooth under the maul of one of the two-leggeds. The imprint on the gene coding was indelible.

Cormac, when he looks for a place to hide because thunder shakes the sky, would crawl into my lap if he'd still fit there. I wondered what that great trembling sound in the heavens represented to him and his kin. If an animal's fear response is triggered by an adversary, what kind of Thing from the Mind of Stephen King could be romping around up there, hidden in those roiling black clouds? And, with this first experience, I just couldn't fathom what had flipped the switch in his head.

Of course, when I told Drew about Cormac's reaction to thunder, he said he doubted it was something new, that I'd only just noticed it.

"Are you suggesting I'm not paying attention to my dog?" I asked.

"No," Drew said. "Anyway, it's kind of a moot point to ponder," he said.

And he was right. There was only the question of what to do about it. I phoned Belle, and asked her what could be done for Cormac. "Can he be trained to get over his fear of thunder?" I asked. She said no, and we talked about the condition, not uncommon among dogs. "I'm sorry, Sonny," she said, "I'm afraid it's Cormac's cross to bear, and something of a thorn in your side."

"Is it that biblical?" I had to smile. "Is there no *salvation* here?"

"Well, if there's such a thing as situational salvation," she replied, "then the answer is yes. There is relief for Cormac and for you." I stood on tiptoes, waiting for her to bring down the tablet from the mount. I almost laughed when Belle offered to write a prescription for "doggy downers." She told me that many pet owners keep a supply on hand.

I was stunned, and told her so. I told her there was no way I was going to turn Cormac into some kind of junkie. She laughed and said such would not become the case. I told her about my doctor asking me to get on medicine to bring my cholesterol down from the stratosphere, how I'd told him I'd get it down my own way, how I ate like a monk and walked two miles a day for six months, how I lost twenty pounds. I told her I wasn't sure that I was trying to bring down my cholesterol, as much as I was trying to stave off being on some pharmaceutical for the rest of my life.

"Did your plan work?" she asked.

"No," I said. "My LDL numbers actually went up after all that."

"So you're on the drugs?"

"I am."

"But you don't want to use drugs on Cormac?"

"No. There are a million thunder boomers that roll across Mobile Bay like Patton's army come to Lower Alabama," I said, and she agreed that living on the Eastern Shore means frequent invasions. "It seems to me," I went on, "when the twentieth, or thirty-seventh, storm occurs without harm, there should come an end to the fear."

"It doesn't work that way," the vet said. "The fear is primal and anti-intelligent."

When I watched the movie *Because of Winn-Dixie*, adapted from Kate DiCamillo's novel, I thought little Opal's preacher dad was surely going to give Winn-Dixie, her newfound dog, his walking papers when he freaked out and transformed into a wild beast during a thunder storm and almost wrecked their mobile home.

But they were committed to the big, rambunctious dog.

They would take care of him no matter what.

Not all dogs, of course, have the phobia. Our neighbor's Golden is completely oblivious to thunder. Bailey sits licking his paws and yawning while his friend from our side of the fence is freaking out.

I thanked Belle for her advice. I told her Cormac and I would work this out drug-free. Somehow. For one thing, I took my electric saw and cut a hole in the garage door and put a kennel crate in there in case I wasn't home when thunder came calling. I put a piece of carpet on the floor and sides of the kennel so it would be quieter and more comfortable. I thought again that we really needed that stronger electronic fence signal. But Ken had said the transmitter was on back order.

Three days later another thunderstorm occurred while Cormac was outside minding the ranch. I waited to see if he'd make his fuss at the back door, and when he did not I went downstairs to check on him. I opened the door to the garage a crack and peeked through. Cormac had used his private door and crate as I'd hoped. I found myself thinking back to the hunting dogs and even the pets I'd known as a child and how all those dogs lived outside. Always. And how maybe I was being too uptight.

TWELVE

I TRY TO IMAGINE what it is like for Cormac when a storm rolls in. Here on the Gulf Coast that telling dark often brings a western sky down on our heads, making Cormac want to crawl inside the pocket of my jeans.

From his point of view, then, let's try this:

My eyes blink open and my body flinches. The reverberation is not audible, it is something I feel in the marrow of my bones, and a shiver runs from my shoulders down my spine and pulls my belly taut. Every hair in my coat seems alive. I leap to my feet and stand on the porch, straining to detect a second pulse from the unseen one dragging its sopping muzzle along the floor that keeps the birds from flying to the moon. There. The thing is now awake and the growl in its chest moves to its voice and the great sound stirs the air like the thrum of a hovering dragon. The hair on my back bristles. My breathing goes faster and faster and my body trembles. My eyes strain in their sockets. I have seen in others of my kind their eyes white-circled with fear of the invisible one. Behind me the door is quiet. No sounds come from inside. Still, I spring against it. My body and legs crash hard against the door, and it rattles and shutters and refuses my plea. I stare at the door. My eyes water but I will not blink. I watch the yellow metal of the round knob and still the door does not open to receive me to safety. The hand that can open the door has been missing for two days. None who live inside are there. All have been missing for two days. Another one with good hands and a good voice has taken their place, but he does not answer my charge on the door. My ear and my neck burn from the impact. I stand on the door, my forepaws extended, and I rake down. My claws tear the wood. Again. And again. The rumble from the animal draws nearer and swings lower, thudding across the hills and tumbling low into the ravines. My breathing burns. It has moved to the tops of my lungs. My mouth is open and my tongue is dry where my hot breath burns across it. My heart is knocking inside my chest. The sky flashes and I know it angers the terrible beast that lives there and the beast will now curse the ones whose paws and hooves and claws hold them to the earth. Perhaps this time he will come to rip open my neck, or tear at my belly. My vision is blurred except at the center of where I look. I drop from the door and spin and look toward the trees. And it comes, the curse flung down on the ground so that it shakes, and the birds must be falling like the water brought by the clouds. When I cry out, my voice breaks inside my throat and a small sound falls from my tongue, but inside my head a red howl is raised and my legs gather beneath me and they release and I run. So that my blood will not soak into the wet soil I run. I run. I run.

THIRTEEN

WE DISCOVERED the intruder the day before I was to go out of town, to fly to San Francisco and begin the book tour for *The Poet of Tolstoy Park*. Cormac and I went around the corner of the house to the garage.

Cormac knew something was up before I did. When I reached down to take hold of the garage door handle and twist it to raise the door, he became excited, jumping from one side of my legs to the other, trying to dash around me.

"Just hold on," I said. He barked, and leaped into the air. "What the—"

When I raised the garage door he dashed inside, barking and racing to the farthest corner. That's when I saw what he was after: a huge brown and gray squirrel sprang from one shelf to another, knocking a gallon of paint to the floor. Of course, the lid came off and pea green paint splattered and spread across the floor. Which, for the moment, I was able to ignore.

The chase was on. I became the kid from Lamar

County, Alabama, who had hunted rabbits with a Long Tom twelve-gauge single-barrel shotgun. I forgot that I was a civilized man. I yelled in a voice that hearkened to my Scottish highlands ancestry, a battle charge cousin Rob Roy would have been proud of.

"Where is he, Mick?!" I flew to the corner where the squirrel was hiding. Cormac actually jumped into the air when the blasted critter ran into view, twitching its tail, chattering. It scampered to a higher shelf.

Did I say I don't like squirrels? A squirrel in a park is okay. A squirrel in my attic or in my garage is not good. I've known them to eat through electrical wiring and start fires in homes. They gnaw rafters. They gnaw holes into air-conditioning ductwork. And, if they had hairless, slick, and gray tails like rats, neither would anyone else like these arboreal rodents (tree rats).

The previous year, squirrels had invaded the attic at either end of my house. They dug into the insulation, down to the ceiling board right above my bed, and above John Luke's bed down the hall. Both of us had to listen to them scurry around up there, their sharp little claws scraping just above our heads. I finally had to go into the attic and remove the gable vents at both ends of the house and toss out their leaves and straw. No, there were no baby squirrels, or big ones, for that matter, at home when I evicted them and their ton of yard debris. Now this squirrel was maybe shopping for new digs in my garage.

"Where is he, Cormac?"

Cormac was up on his hind legs, his forepaws on a bottom shelf. His ears were high and his eyes wide. His tongue wagged out after each time he barked.

"Get the squirrel, Mick!"

But it was hiding somewhere in the assortment of stuff on the shelves, so I grabbed a broom. I don't know if Cormac somehow, according to his hunting dog genetics, equated the broom with a duck hunter's gun, but it was the signal for him to go into really high gear on the squirrel search. Between the two of us, we flushed it from hiding, but neither of us was quick enough to catch it before it made a break into the sunlight outside the open garage door.

I don't know, of course, what we would have done, either of us, if we'd caught the squirrel. It's not a good idea to take a squirrel in hand. Its long incisors can sink easily through flesh and bone. To this day, however, that one brief hunting experience is sufficient for Cormac to go into full retriever dog mode when I say, "Where is it, Mick?" Spoken urgently, those four words get him alert and wide-eyed, standing braced with his tail straight, whipping his head this way and that to spot a squirrel.

Last week, in the car line at school, waiting to pick up

Dylan, I saw a mallard on the little pond just beside the road. "Where is it, Mick?" I asked in a rough whisper. He immediately spotted the duck and went on point. Interestingly enough, he did not bark at all, only froze, standing on the Jeep's back seat, looking out the window, staring out at the duck. Good thing for Mr. Quack we were in the car and there were no brooms in sight.

FOURTEEN

"WHAT SHOULD I DO?" Drew asked. I was quiet. I didn't know what to say. Then I asked how long he'd been missing. "He was here this morning. There wasn't a cloud in the sky when I left and I decided to let him play outside. I got stuck at a job site. There were maybe, what, two thunderclaps before I could get to your place. Then the whole thing passed. It didn't even rain."

I felt as helpless as I'd ever felt. Diana and I were both two thousand miles from Alabama. I'd finished the novel, the publisher had accepted it, and I was on a book tour in San Francisco. Diana would be flying home tomorrow, but I had signings and readings booked in Miami, Atlanta, Nashville, Blytheville, Oxford, Tupelo, Jackson, and New Orleans. I wouldn't be home for ten days.

"Drew, when I asked you to *house* sit," I said, pouring my defeat into the phone, "I wanted you there in my house to watch my dog. The house is not going anywhere. I told you Cormac might panic and bolt if a storm came up."

"Yes you did," Drew allowed. "That doesn't matter now. Let's be smart here," he said. "When Cormac's pulled a breakout in the past, where'd he go? Can I call someone?"

"That's a good idea," I said. "Look up the numbers for Alan Trimble and George Wingfield. They've both got dogs. They live right down the street. I'll dial the message service and see if they've called me."

I phoned to listen to our messages. Diana paced the hotel room, returning again and again to the window to glance toward San Francisco Bay, like there was some news posted out there about Cormac. I sat on the hotel bed and listened to the recordings on our voice mail. Two were from the boys, who were with our friends the Meisters, as though their phone calls to our house would reach us wherever we were; one was from the underground fence man saying the parts for the upgrade had arrived; two were from Pierre who couldn't find certain books for which internet orders had been placed; and the last message was from a woman who did not identify herself, but said our dog had been at her house. Her call had come in an hour and forty-five minutes before Drew phoned me.

Diana sat down beside me. "I should have boarded Cormac."

"Now, Sonny," Diana said, "you've never boarded him.

It's no one's fault Cormac ran away. You know that. He's run through the fence before. It's just that we're not there today. I think we'll find him."

"I shouldn't have left him with Drew," I repeated.

"And do what? Not go on your book tour? That would be silly."

"I *know* that," I said. "But Cormac'll be in Alaska by the time I get home."

"Okay," Diana said, speaking more softly and deliberately. "We are not going to let this devolve into a fight between you and me." She got up and went back to the window again, this time standing and staring through the glass. She turned to me. "I'll be flying home tomorrow. If Cormac's not back—if Drew doesn't find him—the boys and I will go door-to-door in the neighborhood. We'll put up signs. Monday, I'll phone the vets around town. We'll find your dog."

My dog? That was the first time she had referred to Cormac as my dog. I had never called him my dog. I'd thought of him as *our* dog. He shared his company with Diana and John Luke and Dylan, of course, but it was true Cormac had become *my* friend, constantly at *my* side.

Cormac was my first puppy.

Cormac was the only dog since my first dog as a boy who would not get handed off when he became, as my grandmother would say, a "handful." Though never spoken, that had been a vow understood in Jack Bennett's front yard; it had grown into a promise of the heart.

Now with him gone, with this crazy futility pressing down and no reasonable chance that I could go home before this tour was over to look for him, it was plain to me: Cormac had been my dog from the first day I saw him.

And it was I—not my wife Diana, not my sons John Luke or Dylan, not my friend Drew—who had let Cormac down.

Those other times he'd run through the fence, I'd been ignoring him because I was on a single-minded quest to write a book. I stood up and joined Diana at the window. "For some reason," I said to her, "I find myself thinking about Bailey next door. Was he watching when Cormac dashed across the yard, going God-only-knows where?" Did Bailey, I wondered, hear him yelp as he raced through the shock barrier, watch him pick up speed when the thunder followed him?

"*Now* the transmitter thing's there," I said to Diana. "I can't believe I just let that go." This time she didn't have anything to say, only looked away. I went to the closet and got my jacket. I told her I needed to take a short walk. The hotel door closed behind me. I walked to the elevator and pushed the button. I put my hands in my pockets and leaned my shoulder against the wall as I waited.

Down on the sidewalk, I held it all in until I'd gone two blocks.

FIFTEEN

IN ATLANTA, Cormac was still missing. In Nashville, Cormac had not been found. I left Tennessee, headed for Blytheville in Arkansas. My days became a kind of absentminded shorthand between towns, one name on a map to another. I took a detour to drive on the Natchez Trace. I just needed to drive along that pretty road at the 50 mph speed limit.

I did not need to read a book while driving.

But I did.

I held open in my right hand Cormac McCarthy's new book, *No Country for Old Men*. I held onto the steering wheel with my left hand. I set the cruise control at 47 mph and I drove down that pristine highway while I read McCarthy's novel.

I wondered if Mr. McCarthy would be sorry my dog was lost.

While the miles clicked past on the Jeep's odometer, my mind slipped off the road, kept getting all wrapped up in the reddish-brown dog whose absence was a pressure in my chest. I saw him beside me as I drove, his face out the window, speed-reading the wind. I saw him frantically scanning the ground for a leaf to pick up so he could talk to me. I thought of Drew telling me Cormac just wanted to bring me something.

I made my stops at the bookstores, gave my readings, answered questions from the audiences. Cormac was gone now for ten days. From my cell phone, I called the same veterinarians that Diana had already called. I called the Fairhope animal shelter, the dog pound.

To each who answered the phone I repeated: "My name is Sonny Brewer from Fairhope. I'm missing a Golden Retriever, a dark-red male, not neutered, last seen wearing a green electronic collar in the Moseley Road area of Fairhope."

From each who talked to me I got the same answer: "Sorry. We don't have your dog."

I called Drew and asked him to go again to the grocery stores to check the bulletin boards. He said he'd already done that, said he'd also been to the convenience stores where Diana and the boys had taken the missing dog flyers. No luck. I kept driving. I wondered if Cormac was still on the move, too. I did four more bookstores. In New Orleans I told the crowd about Cormac. They had more questions and comments about my dog than about my novel. One lady offered to give me a new dog.

I rolled into my driveway on Good Friday. I spent Easter weekend losing confidence I'd ever get him back. Emily was home from college, staying at her mother's for the weekend. She dropped by on Sunday. "I'm just hoping now," I told her, "that Cormac hasn't been struck by a car and killed."

"Maybe," Emily said, "someone has a new pal for themselves. That's better than what you're thinking."

"Yeah, a handsome reddish-brown doggins of noble lineage and gentle heart," I said. "A good dog."

When the gaggle of kids had had their egg hunt, and Easter Sunday's feast had been eaten and the dishes washed and the tables cleaned, and when all the kinfolk had gone home, John Luke and Dylan came and sat with me on the sofa. I think Diana sent them. One boy on either side of me, a tiny hand on each of my knees, two faces searching mine. I don't remember a time when so much was said without a word being spoken.

"Let's shoot some hoops, guys," I said and stood up. They dashed for the door. When I suggested we play a game of horse, Dylan said, "What about a game of D-O-G? Maybe that will bring Cormac home."

"Sure," I said. "It's worth a try."

"I'll shoot first," John Luke said, dribbling under the goal for an easy layup.

"Daddy," Dylan said, "I'm sorry Cormac is lost."

"Me too," I said.

"Maybe you'll find him before you have to leave again," John Luke said. I had to go back on the road Wednesday.

"He's probably looking for you, too," Dylan said. "And he can find things with his nose."

"He sure can," I said. "We'll just meet in the middle somewhere." Both boys seemed satisfied that would happen. When we went inside I told Diana the boys believed I'd find Cormac.

"Of course they do," she said. "So do I."

After sunset, Diana and I walked out on the back porch. We stood there looking across the yard, listening into the dark. Diana said she'd get the boys ready for bed. I told her I'd be inside soon to tuck them in. When I was alone, way off I heard a dog barking. For a brief moment, I allowed myself to think that it was Cormac, fenced-in in someone's backyard, desperate to get home. But soon enough the night was quiet. Tomorrow, I'd go knock on some doors.

SIXTEEN

I DROPPED THE BOYS at school and went to the bookstore. I'd check in there first, then get down to the business of asking the people down my street for information about Cormac. Pierre and Drew were at the store. Drew shook his head as soon as he saw me.

"Man, I am sorry about Cormac," he said.

"I know," I said. "But don't think for a minute—"

"I don't," Drew said, anticipating that I was about to absolve him. "But I still feel bad it happened on my watch."

"It really didn't, though," I said. "It happened in the months leading up to your watch. I should've stayed on point with the fence people. Maybe I should have got Cormac the doggy downers from Belle."

"Maybe, shmaybe," Pierre said. "Cormac's a dog, fellas."

"More than that to me," I said.

"You know what I mean," Pierre said. "A woman came in here yesterday asking to put up a flyer about her missing cat." He pointed toward the window beside the front door. "Cat. Dog. Whatever. They have minds of their own," he said. Pierre told me every day someone came in to ask about Cormac, had I found him?

Drew agreed. "The network is so wide by now," he said, "wherever he is, he'll be ratted out sooner or later." Both men could tell this line of talk was only going so far with me. Pierre changed tack, told me Eddie Lafitte had come by and left a letter for me.

"About what?" I asked.

"I didn't read it," he said. "What kind of friend do you think I am?" Pierre winked and got the letter from beside the cash register. "You know how Lou is about animals," Pierre said. "I bet it's something about your dog."

"Why wouldn't he just meet me for a cup of coffee?" I asked.

"I don't know," Pierre said. "Just read the letter."

Drew said he was late to meet a plumber at a job site. "Cormac's in the pipeline, pal," Drew said. "Lots of eyes are looking for that red dog. We'll find him." He squeezed my shoulder, nodded to Pierre and left. Pierre said he had to do a couple of book searches online before the customers phoned this morning. I said I'd check back with him later in the day. I looked at the envelope in my hand, wondering what Lou had written.

I first met Eddie "Lou Garou" Lafitte in the company

of Pierre. *Loup-garou* is the French name for werewolf,
and Lou, as his friends call him, is a hairy man. Pierre
said he had a pelt, which was ironic given that Lou had
been a teenage fur trapper in the Louisiana swamps. He
was a Cajun, a six-foot-nine-inch walking book on the
outdoors, had a master's degree in forestry, and had once
hosted his own outdoorsman reality show on cable television. Lou loved dogs everywhere, and particularly
Jenny, his brindled Catahoula. Media people loved *him*,
and he was frequently the authority on some wild creature issue for *Animal Planet* on the Discovery Channel.
Eddie Lafitte narrated a public television special on the
return of brown pelicans to Mobile Bay after nearly a
quarter-century's absence.

Lou's affinity with animals was legend. The day I met
him I watched the legend spread as a scene unfolded
before a group of people seated on the gallery of the Pink
Pony Lounge in Gulf Shores, Alabama, on a certain
sunny Sunday afternoon five years ago.

Pierre had come by the bookstore the previous
Friday afternoon, and asked me to join him and his
friend Lou on Sunday for a ride over to the Gulf beaches,
maybe grab a beer, watch some football on television.

On Sunday, just past noon, Pierre and Lou showed
up. I got into the car with them and we drove south a half
hour until we arrived in Gulf Shores, and went directly to

the Pink Pony. The sun was out, though the wind blew a little chilly. Still, we decided to take our beers to the deck facing the blue waters of the Gulf of Mexico waters. The game between the Saints and the Bears had not yet started. Kickoff was in forty-five minutes.

We were about to sit when I noticed a seagull down at the surf's edge. Weird, it seemed, just sitting there as though hatching an egg. I usually saw seagulls in flight, or running on the beach toward a morsel dropped there by a sunbather, sometimes floating on the waves. I didn't remember seeing one sitting stock-still on the sand.

Lou detected the seagull's broken wing first. He called it to my attention, since he saw me looking in its direction. Even then I couldn't see the damaged wing. But when the bird got to its feet, I saw the short, jagged bone protruding from matted feathers at its left shoulder. "Look at that," I said. Lou said nothing. Pierre asked, "What?"

Then he, too, saw the heavy-seeming and lifeless wing hanging at the gull's side. The bird might have been a child's toy with its gimpy motion. It wobbled along for ten feet and had to sit again. I cut my eyes around to other patrons on the deck. Some were aware of the bird's plight and pointed toward the water's edge, to the gull still sitting on the sand. Some, I could overhear.

"You know," said a small-breasted woman with

straight blond hair to the man beside her who nursed a draft beer in a mug, "you really should do something for that poor bird, Charles."

"Certainly, Jen. And what do you suggest? A quick surgical procedure?" The other couple at their table chuckled. The woman, Jen, was not amused. Charles raised his mug and tilted it, draining the beer down his throat in a single long pull. He set the mug down heavily on the table, and raised two fingers in something like a Boy Scout oath gesture, his proper signal to the waitress that he wanted another beer.

"Must you always be such a jerk, Charles? I asked you a perfectly reasonable question. Is there nothing we can do for that poor bird?"

"No," said Charles. "We'll pretend we're not here and allow the bird to do whatever the bird would do in nature, if, in fact, we were not here. Use your imagination to decide what that would be, Jen."

That was as much as the burly man at my table listened to before slamming down his own beer mug with such energy that it got the attention of everyone on the deck. When he stood, his height commanded authority. No one looked away as Lou hard-booted to the steps that led down to the beach. His footfalls on the board stairs were solemn and heavy.

Out of the windshadow of the Pink Pony, the onshore

breeze whipped Lou's black-and-silver hair and beard. Several yards ahead of the marching Cajun, to his right and just at the water's edge, the bird sat, not even moving when the foaming wave crawled up the beach toward it. Two other seagulls swooped down and congregated on either side of the wounded and disheveled one. The smaller of the two latecomers actually rushed the gull with its broken wing and when it tried to rise to flight it fell, fluttering. The other gull also approached as if to attack. I had never witnessed this kind of behavior among gulls.

The north wind curled over the roof of the bar, down into Pierre's face, blowing his hair around, sending a chill down my back. I drew up my shoulders. Lou slowed his pace as he drew near to the wounded gull. We watched our friend. Everyone watched. There was complete silence on the deck. Only the wind made a small sound, *shushhhh* as it shifted through the chair legs, around the umbrellas.

I wondered if the gull would try to get away from Lou, what he intended to do. By now he stood over the injured bird. It lifted its head, cocked its eye to watch Lou, but otherwise did not move. The big man bent at the waist, his two hands cupped and outstretched. He took the bird into his hands and lifted it to his chest. He stroked its head with his thumb and rocked side-to-side, almost imperceptibly.

"Sweet. Real sweet," Charles said. "I feel a tear welling up."

"Shut up," I said to the man. Pierre also glared at Charles, whose face reddened as he cut his eyes to the man seated at his table, then looked away.

Down on the beach, Lou stopped stroking the seagull, and laid his right palm face-down over its body, as if shielding it from the sun. And, in a motion too quick for me to follow, the giant man closed his right finger and thumb around the bird's head, and with a downward snapping motion, maybe like you'd pop a wet towel, the bird's body thudded against the sand. It flopped a couple of times and lay still. Lou bent down and picked up the gull's body and, turning with an athlete's grace, tossed the head and body far out into the rolling surf. He stood with his back to the gallery for five minutes, still as a figure cast in bronze.

The woman, Jen, got up and walked away from the three people at her table.

Lou did not rejoin us on the deck of the Pink Pony. He angled down the beach in the direction of where we'd parked the car. Pierre and I both put five-dollar bills under our beer mugs and left by the stairs at the side of the deck.

In the five years since that day, Lou and I had become good friends.

I walked across the street, sat in my Jeep, and read Lou's letter, read words the big man could not have said to me in person:

Dear Sonny,

I never know what to say in a time of loss. Everything turns to ashes in my mouth, and words seem so trite and useless. But in such times you are moved to say something the same way you are moved to knot a choking scrap of silk around your neck and squeeze into grown–up shoes and a black coat. It is how we mourn, in Alabama. Sometimes, of course, we also pitch a good drunk, but that is mostly the Catholics.

But we will have no funeral for Cormac, because he is not gone, only lost, and there is a big difference there. Most likely he is not even lost.

He is, I believe, stole.

Somebody saw him, saw his fine red hair and his well-formed body and broad, intelligent head, and stole him. Sons of bitches.

Because Cormac is not a mean soul, he allowed himself to be stole.

Somebody said, "hey boy," and he bounced on over, and was took.

And we are left here to be sorry.

But there some things that need to be said to you

from a friend, and I have never been quiet in my life.

In his days with you and your wife and your boys, he was warm and well-fed and loved as much as any beast can be, and a whole lot better than a lot of children.

He suffered no cruelties. He was not beaten into compliance.

He lived fat and easy in a house on the hill.

The last time I saw him, with you, he literally jumped for joy.

Over and over, he hurled his body into the air, higher and higher.

It almost made me cry.

I had no luck with dogs. The wheels of cars took them, mostly. Fiests, Beagles, mixed-breed hounds, all perished on the Roy Webb Road. The only dog I had for any length of time died from heartworms because I lapsed in my care of him, because I was too busy. I should tell people that when they say nice things about me.

But I had no luck, as to dogs.

So, when you told me how Cormac lay at your feet every single day as you wrote your novel, I was touched but also a little jealous. I am sorry now, for that envy.

Cormac seemed to sense that in me. He followed

me around your house, insisting to be loved on, and when I sat quietly in an otherwise empty room he came in and laid his head on my knee, and just left it there.

Only when he heard your voice did he even twitch, and then he was gone, chasing the sound of your voice up the stairs.

I hope, someday, he just comes walking back up in the yard.

I hope he makes one of those miracle treks home.

I would like to think that whoever took him will have an attack of conscience, but that is unlikely. A man who would steal a dog is a low man, and it may be that all we will ever get from him is a darker satisfaction.

We will learn who took Cormac. We will not kill that man – because even though he is a thief he may have cared for the dog, gently.

But I think we should take him to the swamp. I think we should tie him to a tree, and ask him some questions. We should scare him a little bit.

And if he laughs, or sneers, we will chop off one of his toes.

One of the big ones.

We will take him to the doctor, and leave him in the parking lot, and if he threatens us with legal harm we will remind him that he has nine more toes.

That day, and that satisfaction, may never come. All that is left, in the end, is this.

He was not a lawn ornament, not an animal you bought to be fashionable. He had two acres of trees and fence line to mark as his own, and he did so with great determination. When you left the swimming pool gate open he dove right in, no matter how many times you hollered, "Cormac, damn ye," and chased him out.

He terrorized squirrels and tolerated cats. He woke your two boys up by jumping into their beds. He listened as you read to him from words you wrote. He always, always thought it was fine. He thought you were Melville. He thought you were Faulkner.

He did not, for a big dog, greatly stink.

He loved you back, all of you. You could just tell.

I envy you, still.

Your friend, Lou

SEVENTEEN

THE LADY WHO answered the door immediately asked if I'd come about my dog. Hers was the third house on my rounds that Monday, the 28th of March, with Cormac gone now seventeen days. I didn't know this woman, though I was sure we'd seen each other in the neighborhood.

"Yes, ma'am," I said, wondering how she knew, but withholding hope that she had information I could use. "How did you know? Have you seen him?"

"I know about Cormac because I saw the poster at the gas station just this afternoon," she said. "But he's also been to my house before. I saw your name on his tag the first time he was here. I guess I should have brought him inside. I headed for the phone to call you. As soon as I was out of his sight, though, he went running. So I didn't leave a message. Another time I did leave a message. I think I forgot to say my name, though…which is Ruth Baxter. That was about two weeks ago, maybe."

I wanted to cut her off, to ask her specific questions. I was speaking with someone who'd seen Cormac on the day he took off. It wasn't much, but maybe this was like the first tiny crack in the concrete that lets the green and growing thing poke its head up toward the air and rain and sun. I only had one more day before I had to go back out on the last leg of my book tour.

"Did he look okay? Did he have a collar on? Did you see which way he ran?" I gestured directions left and right with my hands.

"Well, I know where he went to next, so it must've been in that direction," she leaned outside her door and pointed toward the street going away from my house.

"What do you mean, Mrs. Baxter? You know where he went next?"

"Because one of my neighbors—she's got a little wiener dog. I don't have a dog. Or a cat, for that matter," she said. I rolled my hands in a hurry-up-and-get-to-what-the-neighbor-said motion. Diana would've said I was being rude. She would have been right, but at that moment I did not care. Besides, the lady leaning against her doorjamb was oblivious to my lack of good manners. "Anyway, she is Rhonda Perkins, and Rhonda said your dog was at her house the same day I saw it. She said he scared the men who were tending her lawn, and she shooed him away." She fixed me with her gaze. "Is he a mean dog?"

"Hell no," I said. "Of course not."

"Well, Mr. Brewer, you don't have to use profanity at my front door." Her eyes flashed. I was afraid she'd stop helping me.

"I'm so sorry," I said, "You're right. But I've been looking for Cormac and…"

"Then another one of my neighbors," Mrs. Baxter said, completely ignoring what I had said, "—ah, she'd be no help. Anyway, you'll just have to go down the street asking." With that she closed the door.

Two doors down, Rhonda Perkins greeted me warmly. Her Dachshund sniffed my shoes as I stood at her door. "That Ruth," she laughed. "I didn't chase your dog away. In fact, my yardman petted him. I didn't even think to look at his collar for someone to call. Frankly, I forgot." She apologized. I turned and looked toward the street. The morning sun colored and highlighted the broad green leaves of a huge magnolia. Mrs. Perkins's mailbox stood in its cool shade. The lazy scene held no drama at all.

Mrs. Perkins spoke again. "I'm sorry," I said. "I was day-dreaming."

"Florence Weller said she thought she saw a red pickup pass her house that day with a big red dog in the back. Florence lives all the way down at the end of the street. She wouldn't mind at all if you go there and ask about—what did you call him?"

"Cormac," I said, anxious to chase this clue.

"Cormac? Yes, well, that's right. A strange name, though."

Another time I might have given her the story of Irish kings. This time I simply thanked the woman and trotted to my Jeep. When I arrived, Florence Weller already stood on her small front porch.

"Rhonda just phoned to say you'd be down here," Mrs. Weller said. "You must have flown. I'd fly, too, if somebody got my Ralph. I know you must be a mess over losing your dog. I'm so sorry."

"You think you saw him?" I said. I liked the woman right away. "Can you tell me about that?"

"Of course," she said, "I'm sorry. And I don't know if it was your dog I saw in the back of that truck. The dog had long hair and was a dark color, sort of a rusty red, and pretty big. I noticed the truck, a red one, because it was going slow, like maybe it was just starting off. I don't think I've ever seen it on our road. I know I haven't seen it since."

"Which way was it going?" I asked. "Toward town, or the other direction?"

"It was going east," she said, and pointed. "That way."

"Did you say you thought a woman was driving?"

"Oh, I'm certain of that," she said, "though I didn't see her clearly. Lord, do you think she might've been kidnapping your dog?"

"Well," I said, "I don't even know that it was Cormac. I just don't know."

"Did you call the animal shelters?" she asked.

"Yes, ma'am. But I'm going home to call again."

"I expect you'd better do that, Mr. Brewer. I've heard they don't keep animals long at the dog pound." Mrs. Weller saw the shadow that passed across my face, darkening my eyes, tightening my lips. "Oh, I'm sorry. I…"

"It's okay," I said. "I know they put down the dogs there after ten days. But either my wife or I called every day since a week ago Monday when she got home from San Francisco. They say they don't have my dog. Same at all the vet clinics and Fairhope and Daphne city shelters. No one's reported seeing Cormac."

"I will say a prayer for your dog, Mr. Brewer. And for you. I believe you'll find Cormac," she said, and gave me a confident nod. "Cormac? Is that from the writer?"

"Yes," I said. "Not many people guess that."

"I don't know why. Isn't he a wonderful writer? Oh, Blood Meridian just floors me! I've read it three times."

Somehow I took it as an omen that Florence Weller was a fan of Cormac McCarthy. I felt more hope than I'd felt in days. I thanked Mrs. Weller and told her I would phone when I learned something. "Please, Mr. Brewer, if you don't mind. I won't rest until we find him." There was also something comforting to me about the way she'd used that plural possessive pronoun, as though she were right with me on my search for Cormac. I was also glad to have Mrs. Weller's offer of a prayer for my dog and me.

EIGHTEEN

IF IT HAPPENED that a woman in a red truck took him, I can imagine—as Lou suggested in his letter—Cormac was probably ready for companionship. He might have jumped right into the open bed of her vehicle. Perhaps, for him, it was like this:

The voice is easy and it sounds like the one who walks with the little ones where I am fed. But it is not the same voice, so I stop still when it calls a word I have heard and remember, Boy. The one who is inside comes outside and lets down a gate and pats with her hand and says again, Boy. I do not walk, or move. I lift my nose but read only smells of what is outside, nothing of the one with two legs or her places. The voice comes louder. The hands pat and I turn my head toward my shoulder and toward my other shoulder and the one who feeds me is not seen. The voice can take me to the one who feeds me. My tail sweeps and I jump into the place and the hand pats my head and I hear words I know, Good boy.

NINETEEN

I DROVE HOME SLOWLY, encouraged by the little news I'd received of Cormac. It was the middle of the morning and the house was quiet. I went to the study and sat at my desk and opened my notebook with the names and numbers of the shelters and clinics. I started at the top, dialed the number, repeating my mantra to the person who answered: "…Golden Retriever, dark-red male, not neutered, last seen in the Moseley Road area wearing a green electronic collar. He's been missing seventeen days."

And the reply: "Sorry. We haven't seen your dog."

And, from some who recognized my voice: "We still have your phone number, sir. We will call you if he's turned in here."

"I know," I said, "I'm just double-checking. Thanks for your help."

Last place. The dog pound.

"Hi, my name is Sonny Brewer from Fairhope. I'm missing my dog, a Golden Retriever, dark-red male, not neutered, last seen wearing a green electronic collar."

"Yes, sir," the girl said. She sounded fifteen. "We had him. Or, we had one that matched that. Some woman dropped him off, said somethin' about this would be one less dog and a thousand less puppies."

"What? Where is he?" My blood went cold. At the end of a ten-day stay, dogs at this facility were killed by injection. I snatched my feet down from my desktop and leaned forward in my chair.

"Well, sir, I don't rightly know that. I just work here. You'll have to ask up in the office. They're taking in a dog, and I just answered the phone here in the back 'cause I know they're busy. You want me to get somebody?"

"*Now, please!*" My heart beat like I'd done a fifty-yard dash. The next half minute on hold was longer than a day.

"This is Tara Mitchell. May I help you?"

"I'm calling about my dog. The girl...ah—"

"Tiffany Hale."

"Yes, Tiffany said you had a Golden Retriever, a dark-red male..."

"We don't give out information about animals on the phone," she said, her voice flat, final.

"Excuse me, but I've called this place often the last two weeks asking about my dog," I said, feeling the anger begin to burn in my chest and belly, firing up as if from a blacksmith's bellow. "Each time I phoned I was told you didn't have a dog to match that description. But now you're saying—"

"We wouldn't have told you that. We would've told you that you had to come down here and look at the dogs."

"No one told me that. Not once." I exploded. "And right now I don't really give a damn about all that. I want to know about the dog Tiffany Hale admitted you had. I *demand* to know."

"Sir, I will not listen to your profanity. And I will not provide any information on the phone about a dog that we might or might not have ever had here."

"Look, lady—"

"Sir, I've already—"

"Listen! You will tell me what you did with the Golden Retriever you had, or you will tell my lawyer. He'll be calling you back in thirty seconds."

"Frankly, I don't care if you bring the district attorney down here in person, sir." I can hear the woman's voice today as clearly as on that day when she said, "I've been doing this job for four years, and I know what I have to do and I know what I don't have to do. I do not have to tell you anything."

"We'll damn well see about that!" I growled into the phone.

"And I told you about your cussing!" The line went

dead. The woman had hung up.

I phoned Todd Coverdale, my finger shaking so I could hardly press the number to his law office. His secretary answered. My voice broke badly and I had to repeat myself. "I'm sorry, this is Sonny Brewer. May I speak to Todd right away, please."

"Certainly, sir."

"Sonny?" Todd asked. "What's up, buddy?"

I poured it out for Todd, my friend, a lawyer and novelist I'd known for years. He stopped me twice, said slow down. He said he knew Cormac was missing. "But, look, you need to calm down some," Todd sounded truly concerned. "You're going to have a freaking heart attack or something."

"I want you to call the pound for me," I said, my voice breaking. "Tell them we are filing suit right away unless they tell us what we want to know. And I really do want to sue these people."

"Look," Todd said. "You don't want to sue anybody. You want your dog back. I'm not sure Nurse Ratched is going to tell me anything she wouldn't tell you, but we'll give it a shot. Here's what you do. First, relax. Get a breath. Next, drive to my office. Drive slowly, Sonny. Look out the window at cows." Todd's office was in Robertsdale, a small town twenty minutes' drive from Fairhope. "Stop your car and look deeply into the stoned eyes of a cow, man. Calm down."

"I'll be there in twenty minutes," I said.

"Take twenty-five," Todd said.

"This is my dog, Todd."

"I know, buddy. And when you get here, we'll see what we can do."

When I got to Todd's office, he stood out front on the sidewalk. He was wearing neon purple running shorts and gold sneakers and a navy blue sport coat, his hands in the pockets. Looking off down the street in the other direction. Whistling. At the moment, I would have been happier if Todd were wearing chain mail and a horned helmet, a double-edged sword dripping blood onto his muddy hobnail boots. But I'd come this far.

"Good morning, Todd."

He jumped. He looked at me for what seemed a long time, then, dipped his head to me. "Morning to you, Sonny," he said. He looked at his watch. "Good. Twenty-nine minutes. By the way, my book come in?"

I'd forgot that I asked Pierre to order Todd a copy of Robert Penn Warren's *All the King's Men*. He hadn't wanted a first edition, but an older, original hardback with its dust jacket intact. I'd told Pierre maybe a late fifties' Random House printing would *feel* right to Todd.

"I'm sorry, Todd, I don't know. I'm here about something else," I said.

"I know."

"And why are you dressed like that?" I asked.

"I was about to go for a run when you called," he said. "Clear the cobwebs. I've got a big case this week."

"And the jacket?"

"Oh, sort of a nod to 'the doctor is in.' What do you think?" He spread his arms and did a slow turn. I didn't say anything. Todd moved to the door and stood aside. He turned the knob and swung the door inward. "After you," he said. I walked into the reception area. The woman behind the desk nodded.

"Dora, hold my calls, please."

"Yes, sir," she said, and then looked at me. "May I get you coffee, or a beverage, sir?"

"No, but thank you."

"Come in, Sonny. Let's see what we can do," Todd said. This time, he went ahead of me, into his office and around the big rosewood desk to sit in a high-back antique swiveling chair with a worn plaid cushion on the seat. The moment he was seated, facing me, so I could not see his running shorts and sneakers, his entire demeanor seemed to shift to that of a confident, competent barrister.

"Now, tell me again what's happened so far," Todd said. "Take it from what the woman on your street told you."

I told Todd the story, right up through the morning's

events and what the lady at the dog pound had said to me. "So, I'm hoping you can call down there and find out what they did with the dog that might be Cormac. Maybe you can get whatever information they have."

"Let's just see, shall we?" Todd told me he found the dog pound manager's behavior odd, but didn't foresee taking the matter to the law, then repeated himself, "Let's just see."

I opened my notepad to read out the phone number to Todd. He had already looked it up and was dialing. "Yes, hello. This is Todd Coverdale. May I please speak to Tara Mitchell?" He spun his chair to face the window to his right, and rubbed the top of his head, mussing his hair so that it was now every which way. "Ms. Mitchell, my name is Todd Coverdale. I am an attorney in Robertsdale."

He took a breath and turned his chair back toward me. "Today, I'm calling on behalf of Sonny Brewer who would like information on a Golden Retriever your employee Tiffany Hale told him you recently had on your roster there." Todd listened into the phone, stood up and walked to the window, his back to me.

"Well, Ms. Mitchell, I would prefer for you to tell me if you think you had a dog to match the description of Mr. Brewer's dog, and tell me where that dog is now, as far as you know." Todd paced back and forth in front of the big window. "Yes, but we will be back in touch, I assure you." Todd held the phone away and pushed the off button on the handset.

"She wouldn't tell you anything?" I asked.

"Curiously enough, no she would not," Todd said. "She was pretty high-strung in her refusal. I cannot imagine, for the life of me, why she wouldn't give out information on a dog that, by admission of an employee, they boarded at one time." He looked away and rubbed his head again.

"Now what?" I asked, holding my voice steady. But my face must have conveyed my sense of urgency

"I've got a friend who is past president of the Canine Society," he said. "I'll give Phyllis a call right now." The woman's refusal to tell him anything had kindled Todd's interest. He phoned his friend, and matter-of-factly told her what I'd said, and what his experience had been. "Do you know this Tara Mitchell?" Todd asked his friend. "That might help. So, you'll give her a call now, then? Good. Sonny and I are in my office. We'll wait for you to phone back." Todd smiled reassuringly and sat down. "I expect Phyllis will get the information. She's worked with this woman before."

I thanked Todd for his help, told him I'd also check his book order with Pierre. Todd wanted to know how it was going with sales of my novel. I told him things were going great until this had happened. I asked him about his books. He said his last book sold well, and there was a movie deal working on a book he'd written three years earlier.

"*The Poet of Tolstoy Park* is next beside my reading chair," Todd said. He told me he normally had three or four books going, but that he would do me the courtesy of reading mine without company. I looked at the framed covers of Todd's books hanging on one wall of his office.

"You know," I said, "I've looked forward to this for a long time. Getting a book published. Actually, reaching back to college writing classes. But it's hard to enjoy the book stuff with my dog missing," I said. "I've thought about Cormac almost by the minute since I got the call from Drew. Every time I see a Golden I do a double take and my mind starts spinning again. I've even dreamed about him. My boys have asked me a hundred times 'Where is Cormac?' They've both cried about him."

"Let's see if we can't get some news about the Golden at the dog pound," Todd said. "It may not even be your dog," he cautioned, "but we'll take first things first."

The phone rang. Todd reached to answer it, then stopped. "I'll let the secretary get it," he said, "in case it's not my friend." But right away the intercom on Todd's desk buzzed and the secretary said Phyllis Blake was on the line. He leaned forward and took the call. His face immediately sagged, then drew into a frown. "Whatever you can do," Todd said.

"Nothing?" I asked.

"I'm afraid not, Sonny. But Phyllis said she'd drive down to the dog pound later this afternoon to see if she can influence Ms. Mitchell to tell her what she knows."

"What is this woman's problem?" I asked, as much of the floor and ceiling as of Todd. "Something's just not right about all this." I stood up. "I'm going down there myself! She's crazy if she thinks I'm just going to drop this."

"Look, Sonny," Todd said, quickly coming to his feet behind his desk. "I'm going to advise you not to go to the dog pound. I don't think there's anything 'going on,' as you suggest. I think you simply got on the wrong side of Ms. Mitchell at the outset, and as soon as she cools down a bit she'll tell my friend what we want to know. I think if you go down there—at least right now—there's a good chance it'll just make things worse."

"But, this is ridiculous, Todd! Who does she think she is? What's the point of her behavior?"

"I'm sure I don't know. But look, I give you my word that if we don't hear something this afternoon, I will personally ride down there with you in the morning. How is that?" Todd assured me this would stay at the top of his screen until we got answers.

"If you don't call me this afternoon, Todd, I'll be here at 7:30 in the morning. Is that too early?"

"Oh no. I'm at the office before seven every morning. And try not to worry. We'll get to the bottom of this."

I walked out of Todd's office unable to bring things into focus. I couldn't be confident that they hadn't put down the dog Tiffany Hale said had been there. I could think of no good reason for Tara Mitchell to resist giving a simple answer to the question, "Where is the dog now?"

All my intuition told me it had been Cormac there at the dog pound. All my fears told me that I was too late to get him back.

TWENTY

WHILE I WAS AWAY on tour, Pierre mentioned to everyone who walked into the bookstore that my dog was gone. Diana had brought copies of the reward poster to him. He'd made additional copies and handed off a flyer to anyone willing to take it and post it somewhere meaningful.

Before going inside the bookstore, I stood out front and looked at the face of Cormac on posters in the windows on either side of the red French door. The photo of Cormac had been taken months ago, a shot of him lying on the floor between John Luke and Dylan, with the boys cropped out, though John Luke's hand could be seen draped over Cormac's side. The vet had told Diana to be sure to eliminate the boys' faces from the reward poster, that child welfare agencies warned against putting kids' pictures out like that. I looked at the picture there, however, and saw the whole unedited scene: two boys and a dog posing for the camera, stretched out laughing on the carpet. Emotions churned in me, and I thought if I didn't just go ahead and bawl, I'd throw up on the sidewalk.

I must have been telegraphing my feelings of utter hopelessness, because when Lou swung open the French door and stepped from inside the bookstore across the threshold in my direction with his hand held out, he looked like he was reaching for a drowning man. And there could have been no more blessed sight, at that moment for me, than that big man's hand reaching for me. Like Rubeus Hagrid, Harry Potter's gentle giant, Lou Lafitte looked, indeed, twice as tall as any man.

What I did not expect was that right there on the sidewalk he would also become wild and more deserving than ever of his nickname. It seemed to me his salt-and-pepper mane and beard turned red with anger as I told him of my morning's frustrations.

"Come with me, Sonny." Lou walked me to his truck, patted his Catahoula standing in the bed, a fierce leopard-looking dog. He held the passenger door open for me. Lou took charge, as though he knew that was what I needed then, that I was mostly out of ideas. I sat in the truck and was drawn into a certain fold of comfort and security. Lou got behind the wheel. Before he started the engine he put his broad palm on my shoulder, and gave me a little shove that was reassuring. I looked out the truck window and saw Pierre running across the street.

"Hello, Sonny. You're not coming inside to tell me what you think, mon ami? The place looks good." Pierre spread his arms. "I want you to see how I've rearranged shelves and moved around the sofa and chairs."

"Later with the Martha Stewart crap!" Lou barked, and shook his hand at Pierre to get back from the truck. "What's the phone number at the dog pound?"

I reached into my vest pocket for my small black moleskin journal, held it up and flipped off the elastic band that held the front cover closed. I thumbed it open to the page of phone numbers for the clinics and shelters I'd been checking with. I gave Lou the number at the dog pound. He poked the buttons on the handset with force enough to jar it with each number. His eyes were fierce, looked across a million miles. He stood alone on the planet, save for some distant figure he drew into focus.

"Tara? This is Lou Lafitte. I know you, and you know me," he said into the phone. "You had my friend's dog down there. Now you're about to have me down there looking for answers. I'll be there in five minutes. Clear your calendar."

Lou started the truck's engine and sped away from the curb.

"Don't spill Jenny," I warned.

"You couldn't dynamite that leopard dog out of the bed of this truck," Lou said. "Besides, her collar's leashed to the floor back there. She can range to the side bed, but no farther. It's a good system that everybody's dog in an open pickup should have."

"I know," I said. "Belle told me all about it."

Lou didn't exceed the speed limit, but I had the sensation of traveling at the speed of light. Lou said little. I said nothing. Once I started to tell Lou that Todd Coverdale said don't go to the pound, but let it go. When we got there I would let Lou do all the talking.

Fifteen minutes later we pulled into the gravel parking lot of the pound. Lou was out the truck door while it still rocked from the drive and the motor still coughed. He didn't wait for me. He did, however, pat Jenny and tell her to stay. I debated staying put, to heed my lawyer's advice, a debate that ended in ten seconds. The door was ajar to Tara Mitchell's office. When I walked in, I heard, "…what it feels like to read about yourself on the front pages of America's daily newspapers. I know just about all the editors, Tara, from Chicago and San Francisco to New York and Atlanta." I stepped into her office. The woman he addressed displayed none of the authority she had wielded so freely on the phone with me. She was pretty, dressed in tight khaki pants, with her brown hair in a ponytail. While she did not by any means cower from Lou, neither did she oppose him.

He barreled ahead. "Not one of those editors would

turn down a story about a man and his dog. Especially when that man acknowledged his dog at the front of his novel and lost his dog while touring that very book." Tara Mitchell looked at me, then back at Lou, whose big chest swelled when he pulled in a breath. "You've got sixty seconds to tell me about the Golden Retriever you had in your cages. I'm not threatening you, *cher*, just telling you what a nightmare it'll be for you to field questions from CNN rookie reporters. You don't want to know how bad a newsman's breath smells when he starts panting to make a name for himself." If Tara had some reply, she didn't have a chance to give it as Lou trundled onward.

"You don't know slime, Tara, 'til you've been slimed by snakes ready to swallow you whole in the name of free press. You screwed up in your job at the dog pound, or at a New Year's Eve party. Once or six times. You do not want those mistakes indexed on your own TV program listings. But I'll make sure that's what happens."

Lou huffed another deep breath. "Now you've got ten seconds."

I blinked like a man caught in a dust storm, trying to block the tears. My breathing had moved so high in my lungs I felt I might suffocate. And when Lou snatched a pen from his shirt pocket, my heart jacked in my chest like an air chisel hammering through concrete and rebar. He scribbled onto one of the note pads on the counter.

"And maybe you've got a green collar somewhere in this rat's nest on your desk. I'll be taking it with me when I go." Lou had forgotten to return my cell phone to me, and noticing its bulge in his shirt pocket, he fished it out and tossed it to me. He fixed his eyes on me, rage still smoldering the coal-black shine of them.

Tara Mitchell bent over her desk, found a pen, and wrote something down on a pad. She tore off the sheet of paper. "This is the name of the man who picked up the Golden last Monday. This is his cell number."

Lou handed the piece of paper to me. "This is your call to make, friend," he said. He looked back at Tara Mitchell. "If he crawfishes, he'll get the same deal I offered you. Call him when we step out of your office, Tara. Promise him that Lou Lafitte will deliver." He smacked his big palm down on the desk, startling the woman and me. "Now, photocopies of the paperwork on the Golden Retriever and the collar." He turned his face to me. "You'll know your collar, right?"

"Absolutely," I said.

"I don't have it," Tara Mitchell said. "I'll make copies for you, but the collar's been missing from my office since the day after the Golden was taken." She opened a file drawer and took out papers, made copies and handed them to Lou.

"I'm going to take Mr. Brewer back to Fairhope, Tara.

I'll be back down here in one hour. Maybe before I get back you'll find the collar," the big man said, and stalked toward the door. He stopped still in his tracks when he realized I was rooted to the floor. Lou turned, walked back to me, and bent to wrap his arms around me.

"Maybe your dog ain't gone for much longer," he said, like a grandfather would say to a grandson needing a boost of confidence. I tossed in the towel at that point, and shed some tears as manly as I could, my head up, my shoulders square, my face pretty quickly turning into a wet mess. He stood back nodding, my eyes caught in his. "Not to worry," Lou said, and we headed for the door. Tara Mitchell actually stepped forward as I passed and gave me a light tap on the shoulder.

When we got to his truck, Lou took a minute to talk to his dog. Most of Jenny's tail-thrashing, wiggling excitement had shifted to an interest in me, whether I was friend or foe. Lou opened his door. He reached under the driver's seat and tossed me an oily rag. I wiped my eyes and blew my nose.

"Keep it," he said. "I've got more at home."

TWENTY-ONE

PIERRE INVITED ME to take the cordless phone back into the kitchen. "For privacy," he said. I knew that he also intended that I leave any customers who might stop by out of this. I think he feared I might get cranked up the way I told him Lou had at the dog pound. I feared he was right.

"You know," I said to Pierre as I took the phone from him, "it dawns on me that the papers show this dog was handed off on the 21st of March. If it turns out it's Cormac, that day would have been his fourth birthday. What a sorry sense of humor on the part of the Great Spirit of All Dogs."

"Unless you count that the dog pound didn't kill him on his tenth day in the pokey," Pierre added. That stopped me. I felt a shiver with goose bumps following. I stood holding the phone, staring at it as though some oracular voice would crackle from it and offer me a navigational fix in the heavens, some bright star to give me a reference point in this weird, loopy course I stumbled along.

"You're right," I said, my voice low. "You know, Pierre, how I claim nine as my lucky number?" He nodded. "When I thought about this birthday coincidence I added together the string of numbers in the date of Cormac's birthday: 3-21-2001. It comes to nine. Maybe there is some luck running here. And, maybe, just maybe, this man I'm about to call will help me sort out some things."

"If you get lucky, it'll be because you've worked hard for it," Pierre said. "I don't have a dog. But if I did, and if he ran away, I'm thinking I'd say something like, 'Fido was a good old dog.' And that would be that. Your dog thing is different. You're earning every drop of luck you get."

"And you and Lou are helping me," I said.

"That's because we are your friends," Pierre said.

"Well, I'm grateful. You know that, I hope," I said. Pierre waved off my remark, and said nothing. I held up the papers. "Something else here that's mighty interesting. Suspicious, even," I said.

"What?"

"The dog's name on this paperwork is Cognac," I said. "That sounds a lot like Cormac, don't you think?"

"Now that's a lot weirder to me than that hooha about the numbers," Pierre said. "No way that's coincidental."

"I think you're right," I said. "Makes me more confident it's my dog I'm chasing here."

I closed the door into the tiny kitchen, held up the scrap of notepaper that I'd involuntarily crumpled in my left hand. I unwadded it and put it on the counter beside the coffee pot. I looked around for a stool, but decided instead to stand. *Stand and deliver*, I thought. I took a long, slow breath, and keyed in the number for a Mr. Clyde Grossett. He answered on the second ring.

"Hello, Mr. Grossett."

"Yes."

"My name is Sonny Brewer from Fairhope."

"Yes. So, how may I help you, Mr. Brewer?"

"You took a Golden Retriever from the dog pound last Monday." My pulse was already beginning to race as my heart kicked into fight-or-flight mode. I had zero control of it.

"Ah, yes," he said, his voice telling me that Clyde Grossett was proceeding with caution.

"I have reason to believe that was my dog," I said. "I lost my Golden about two weeks ago. I'd like to come look at him. May I?"

"Well, Mr. Brewer, I'm afraid that's not possible. He is not with me."

"Where is he?"

"I'm not able to provide that information, sir."

"Why the hell not?" I asked, trying to speak from the same platform of authority occupied only minutes ago by my friend Lou Lafitte. Only thing, my balance seemed questionable and I felt a wobble underneath me. Lou had stood tall and wide, like a pirate captain aboard his flagship.

"Let's keep this civil, Mr. Brewer. I am a member of a Golden Retriever rescue network. That dog was processed and interfaced with the system. He is no longer local."

"Processed? Interfaced? No longer local?" I was livid. I shouted into the phone, "What are you even talking about? Just tell me what you did with the dog you picked up." Pierre walked into the kitchen, stood just inside the open door looking at me. His face was flat, serious. My hand shook.

"I've already told you, sir. I don't have the information you seek," said the thin voice on the phone. "And I am about to terminate this call. But should I continue this dialogue, Mr. Brewer, I would have serious questions for you about why you lost him in the first place. Why are you only now taking this up? By your own admission it has been more than two weeks—"

Pierre snatched the phone from my hand. "Excuse me, Mr.—" Pierre's eyes found the piece of notepaper with the name and phone number on it. He touched it with his index finger. "Mr. Grossett. I am Pierre Fouchere, an associate of Sonny Brewer. Tara Mitchell at first refused to share your contact information with us. She changed her mind. The reason she changed her mind is the same reason you will change your mind. You have three minutes to call Tara Mitchell and return this call to me." Pierre held the handset at arm's length, and with a swirl and flourish, punched the button to end the call.

"Now, we are three. *Musketeers*, we! On a mission to save Fido." Pierre sang. He plucked a butter knife from the dish drain, and carved big curving figures in the air in front of my face. He spun and with a faltering war cry drove the butter knife into a loaf of bread still inside its plastic sleeve, which served to prevent the blunt knife from actually piercing the wrapper, more or less mashing the loaf instead. Pierre dropped his weapon and delivered a crushing karate chop, completely smushing the bread. I cannot judge whether it was the comedic content of Pierre's routine, or the desperation choking me like a python, or some combination of both, but I doubled over in delirium and laughed so hard it seemed to frighten Pierre. As though something in me had snapped.

I was still laughing when the phone rang.

Pierre snapped to attention like a soldier surprised by a general, quickly putting his finger to his lips, shushing me loudly, which also blew out the flame of humor we'd kindled. I stood up straight. Pierre answered the phone.

"Pierre Fouchere." He kept his eyes on me as he listened into the phone. "Hold on, I'll ask you to repeat that." Pierre asked me to write some things down. I took out my moleskin journal and opened it to a clean page. I told him to go ahead.

"Boulevard Animal Clinic in Mobile," Pierre repeated, and called out a phone number. I took dictation. "Golden Love in Danbury, Connecticut," he continued, and called out another phone number. Pierre listened for another minute, and then said, "You saved yourself a great deal of trouble, Mr. Grossett. And here's some advice: rewrite your rescue mission statement, pal, and add a first line in all caps about making an effort to reunite pets with owners. If I need anything else, I'll call."

Pierre stood, silent, shaking his head. "It's a Golden Retriever pipeline," he said, and told me that Clyde Grossett had picked up the dog Tiffany Hale told me about, and had taken him to Mobile to a veterinarian clinic where his *processing* amounted to a checkup, shots, and neutering.

"And, then, because of some, what, supply agreement with a Golden Retriever outfit in Connecticut, shipped him there for adoption." Pierre said he couldn't figure that one out. "Grossett said you'd find out that the dog he 'put through' was too young to be yours," he said. I'd told Tara Mitchell my dog was four.

"Was the dog carrying a license?" I asked, my anger still simmering. "How do they know how old it was?"

"You've got to get to the bottom of this, Sonny," Pierre said.

"At the bottom of this is getting my dog back. That's all," I said. "I've got no interest in some kind of suburban intrigue swirling around 'the woman in the red truck' or even knowing one more thing about this goofy Grossett and whatever deal he might have with the dog pound."

"Well, I do!" Pierre said. "And Lou does. We'll be your Sherlock Holmes and Dr. Watson. Sounds like these rescuers might rescue a dog from the edge of its own yard."

"You two go for it. And keep me posted," I said. "I just want Cormac back home." I told Pierre I wanted to take this one step at a time, with one goal in mind: find Cormac. And that the next step was a phone call to this Boulevard Animal Clinic, then Golden Love, a Golden Retriever 'adoption' agency in Connecticut.

"Okay," Pierre said, "let me leave you to your work."

What I learned at the clinic was pretty clinical, that they performed routine exams on "rescues" for a number of organizations, that they gave shots, neutered, and spayed. When I asked about the specific Golden Retriever they had on March 21, one week ago, they put me on hold, found the paperwork, then read to me from his chart, tellling me the dog was called Cognac. I had this flash that if this was Cormac, then there was at least some measure of familiarity for him in the name by which he

was being called. It wasn't much, but it gave me a bit of a
lift.

The dog they'd seen was a healthy young male. He
was treated to a round of appropriate shots, neutered on
the 21st and released on the 23rd to "authorized individ-
uals" who processed him to the next step. Easy for you to
say, I thought, but where'd they get their authority? I
thanked the receptionist.

I punched in the number for Golden Love and got a
recording.

"Thank you for calling Golden Love, an adoption
agency for Golden Retrievers, and Golden Retriever-
mixed dogs. Please leave a message, or call back to
arrange an appointment to visit with one of our adopt-
able Goldens. We will return your call right away. You
may drop in at our office at any time, of course, but our
special dogs are not on the premises. They are in the
loving care and keeping of temporary foster families
while they wait to find their forever homes. Thank you
and have a golden day."

The knot in my stomach did not digest well the
syrupy sweet message on the phone. I chose not to leave
a message and would call again in half an hour. I put
away my cell phone and went to the front of the bookstore. Pierre was with a customer, showing an album
page of baseball cards at the counter. I put my hand up as

I walked past. He excused himself to the customer, and asked, "No luck?" He could read the answer on my face, but I still said no.

"I'll be back in a bit to catch up with Lou, see what happened on his second trip to the pound," I said. "If he's got the collar, that'll end the speculation about whether or not Cormac's in Connecticut."

I had promised Belle I'd let her know as soon as I found Cormac or got news of him. I decided to go to her clinic and talk to her. I sat in her waiting room, visiting with a big Old English Sheepdog, whose owner introduced him as Newton. After a few minutes, Belle stuck her head around the corner and invited me back. When I'd told her the whole story, all that I knew so far, I asked her a question. "What's with shipping the dog to Connecticut?" I told her Grossett had used the phrase *put through*, to describe his handling of the dog he picked up.

"That's the problem, Sonny," she said, and went on to tell me she didn't think there were bad guys in this, no dog Nazis, she said. "I think you're dealing with people overcome with zeal to rescue a certain breed. When they keep a dog from dying at a pound, that's good, of course. But, there should be a matching effort to return dogs to their owners." She told me the expense and effort to "process" dogs could also include trying to reunite lost dogs with owners.

"I mean, look at this dog they 'put through.' He was sporting a two-hundred-and-fifty-dollar collar," Belle said. "Does that sound like an abandoned animal? But the rescue outfits never call me at the clinic. Not once has the likes of this Grossett fellow phoned us hoping to put a dog back with its owner. It really tees me off." I'd never seen Belle so upset.

"And why Connecticut?" I asked. "That's a long ride for a dog from Alabama."

She told me she could only guess. "If they've got expensive fines for having pets that aren't neutered or spayed, and, on the other hand, a breeder's license is also expensive, then one consequence of those laws could be a shortage of some breeds. Maybe Golden Retrievers are a scarcity in Connecticut."

She told me I could research the internet for other ideas, but I told Belle I didn't want to write a paper. "I just want my dog back."

I knelt to pet one of the office cats wandering around, a big Calico female. I looked up at Belle. "You know," I said, "the woman on my road who thought she saw Cormac in the back of a red pickup also said she'd heard of people who will take a dog from its own yard and turn it over to a rescue network. Pierre has the idea that the driver of the red truck might be someone who collects dogs and turns them over to the pound."

"A person who would do that has some pretty serious problems," Belle suggested. "Did you try to find out who was the owner of the red truck?"

"No," I said. "Not yet. But, I've seen a million red trucks this morning. I wouldn't know where to start. Pierre said he and Lou will find her before they drop the case."

Belle smiled and held out her hand as I stood. She called my attention to the bulletin board behind me. Push-pinned there were more than a half-dozen flyers for missing dogs, even another Golden Retriever, last seen two months earlier. She told me she didn't hold out a lot of hope for good results from flyers. Belle patted my shoulder. "You just stay on the trail of your dog," she said. "That's the best use of your time now."

I told her I thought she was right, and I had one more question. "The vet in Mobile doesn't believe they had Cormac. They said the dog they saw had teeth too clean and white for a four-year old."

"Oh, poppycock," she said. I'd never heard anyone say that except in movies. "Cormac had beautiful teeth because you fed him a proper diet and kept him supplied with chew toys. A dog's teeth," Belle said, "are a good tool for estimating age. Same with horses. But that's all. This fellow with the shiny white teeth could still be Cormac."

Then she asked me if I was going to fly to Connecticut

to identify the pooch.

"I don't know," I said. "If I have to I will. I'll ask for some digital images, have them emailed to me tomorrow from this Golden Love agency. But I'm afraid I wouldn't be any more certain it's Cormac by looking at a picture than the vet can be certain of his age from looking at his teeth."

Belle agreed. Then she became more the doctor. "When you get him back—and I think you will, even if this isn't him—you'll bring him to the clinic and let me put a chip in him." It wasn't a question. She was giving me instructions. I told her I would without hesitation. She didn't lecture me about having asked me once before to get Cormac chipped. Belle was gracious like that, probably knew this was on the list that added up to the load of remorse I felt.

"Oh," I said, getting up to go, "you know what name they used for the Golden they put through?" She shook her head. "Cognac," I said. "Doesn't that sound suspiciously like Cormac? What really bothers me, Belle, is the possibility that the collar Tiffany Hale mentioned still had his ID tag on it. If someone read Cormac there, called him that and it was heard as *Cognac*, that would explain where they got the name. Right?"

"Sounds like a fair call," she said. "But who would have removed Cormac's tag from the collar? And, why?"

"*Why* I don't know. *Who* could be anyone, even Tiffany at the pound. I don't want to make accusations, but it bothers me, naturally, that someone could have also read my name and phone number on the other side of that tag and Cormac could have been spared all this."

"That would bother me, too," she said.

"Maybe even make you really angry?" I asked. Belle nodded. "And so am I. But, I'll get over it when I get Cormac back with me."

TWENTY-TWO

I THINK ABOUT CORMAC carted off by strangers. I think about those words on the cover of the book from Mr. Bennett: I will take care of you. I think of those words fading beneath some sorcerer's wicked grin, his bony hand waving over the book. And if by magic I could know what was in Cormac's head, it might go like this:

There is pain, but there is not room inside this box to turn. I cannot lick the wound, but the pain is less each day, and so it will go soon. There are others like me, in other boxes like mine. It is dark inside here, and the box moves and shakes as we go. The one who feeds me and walks with me and calls out to me, the one to whom I run, he does not put me in a box. I could see him beside me when I rode before and I could see trees and the world and I could smell a thousand smells in one breath. When I rode before we would go and come back to my bed and bowl and the hand that put the food touched my head and his voice called in the morning. The hands and voices and the smells are not the same now. My muscles tremble and I wait.

TWENTY-THREE

LOU MET ME back at the bookstore. He was empty-handed, no collar. But he said he was satisfied there was nothing weird going on between the dog pound and Grossett.

"Tara told me she calls Grossett when they get a Golden Retriever, and at the end of a ten-day stay, he's allowed to come and take them. She said it's one less dog she has to put down." Lou told me she had no apology for stonewalling me. "She's a hard woman who doesn't really like her job. And who would?" he asked.

I quizzed Lou again about the collar.

"Tara said she couldn't find it," Lou said, "and I believe her when she says she doesn't know what happened to it." I told Lou about the name Cognac for the Golden they had processed northward.

"The papers listed his name as Cognac, which sounds a lot like Cormac," I said. "But, you know, there are a thousand more questions, most of which I'd ask the woman who delivered the dog to the pound. But I can't stop every woman I see driving a red truck."

"Right now, let's find out if the dog in Connecticut is Cormac," Lou said. "All our detective work comes to rest about twelve hundred miles north of where we're standing."

"You should just go," Pierre chimed in.

"Is that your plan?" Lou asked.

"That's Plan B," I said. "Plan A is to talk to the people at Golden Love Agency in Connecticut. I'm sure they have photos they can email to me. There are some questions I can ask that might convince me it's Cormac."

"We aren't getting any younger, Sonny. Let's be asking the questions," Lou said.

I agreed and both men followed me outside where I sat at the small marble-top café table on the sidewalk beside the front door. The March sun was warm in the light breeze that played down the street. Lou ducked his head beneath the Over the Transom sign and took the other chair, a good solid cast aluminum chair in the style of wrought iron filigree that could bear up under his weight. Pierre stood, his shoulder propped against the doorjamb. He had his eye on a pretty woman strolling along the sidewalk on the opposite side of the street.

I pushed redial on my cell, and the phone began ringing at Golden Love. "Good morning, Golden Love," a young woman's voice said. I looked at my watch. They had a half hour of morning left in Connecticut.

"Good morning. My name is Sonny Brewer. I'm in Fairhope, Alabama."

"Oh, Mr. Brewer, we've been expecting your call. Let me get my supervisor. Hold the line for me please." I waited for thirty seconds, each tick-tock deep in the workings of my wristwatch stretching into untold time.

"Hello, Mr. Brewer. My name is Fenton Jones. I'm the director of Golden Love Rescue Agency. How may I help you, sir?" My first thought was he already knew what I wanted if he had expected my call. Grossett had surely alerted them.

"I lost my Golden Retriever a couple of weeks ago. I believe he may have been processed into your agency," I said, using their own jargon. "A dog matching the description of mine was pushed through from Mobile, Alabama, released from Boulevard Animal Clinic on the 23rd. His name is Cormac, but the name on his paperwork might be Cognac."

"Yes, it's Cognac. And let me say right away, sir," said Fenton Jones, "that if Cognac is Cormac, then we want to get him back to you as soon as possible. We'll discuss those details if that is in order, Mr. Brewer. Our foster family has agreed to speak to you. Mrs. Erma Blessing is waiting for your call now." The director slowly recited her phone number to me. My hand shook as I took down the information. Pierre had stopped watching the woman stroll down the street, and Lou leaned toward me, his giant arms bent, his elbows resting on his knees.

"Thank you. I'll call you back very soon." I flipped my cell phone closed. I released my breath. I looked from Pierre to Lou, and gave them a thumbs-up. "Finally, I'm talking to a dog-lover. I can just tell. Now, let's see what Erma Blessing can tell me about her foster doggins."

As soon as she answered, Erma Blessing said, "Mr. Brewer, the word's gone around that you are a very angry man. I don't blame you. But do not talk mean to me, or I will hang up and I will not answer your call back."

"Yes, ma'am," I said.

"I open my home to the dogs that need a temporary good home," Mrs. Blessing said. "I am paid for their food. That is all. I do this because I love dogs. I have six of my own." She paused, and I could hear her take a breath. "Now," she went on, "what can I tell you about this good-looking fellow at my feet?"

"Ah—" I could not think of a thing to say. I could not think of a question to ask. "Ah, let me see." I smiled. "Okay. What does he look like? Is he dark red?"

"Yes."

"Okay. Is he about, say 75 pounds?"

"He's kind of skinny. I don't think so. But this fellow has been on quite an adventure, I'm told."

"Ah—let's see." I shook my head. "Oh I know, does he put one back leg underneath the other when he's lying on his side, so that his other leg is kind of cocked up in the air?"

She laughed. "I haven't noticed that," she said. "Now, Mr. Brewer, I can send you some photos. My husband would have to take them when he gets home from the office."

"He loves to take things in his mouth and, well, make these noises as though he's trying to speak," I said. Pierre and Lou liked that one.

"That's a match!" Erma Blessing said. "This fellow will make his sounds around the tiniest thing he picks up. A plastic straw this morning he found on the ground outside was quite sufficient." I turned loose of the hope I'd held in check and let it spill the way I'd spilled raw anger earlier.

"That's it! I've got it," I said in a rush. "Can I talk to him?"

Erma Blessing laughed. "We do that, too," she said. "My husband and I talk to our dogs. It drives my son crazy, and he wants to hide if we do it in public. Yes, Mr. Brewer, here I'll hold the phone for him. He's here in the kitchen with me."

I called Cormac by name, going high and falsetto, down low, growly, calling him Mickins, Cormac, Mick.

"Are you my doggins?" Pierre and Lou looked away from me with their eyebrows cocked high. They slipped a glance at each other and sniggered.

Erma Blessing, on the other hand, came back on the phone, sobbing. "Mr. Brewer, this is surely your dog. This must be Cormac! He is on the floor with eyes like the moon, his face between his paws. Forgive the allusion to advertising nostalgia, but I do believe he's heard his master's voice."

I leaped from my chair at the table, did a pirouette, yelling. Pierre and Lou did a high five and clapped me on the back. "I know what I told you, man," said Lou, "but I don't believe this. I cannot believe you found the mutt!"

I calmed myself, got back on the line with Erma Blessing. I walked down the sidewalk with my cell phone to my ear, listening as she told me how they'd spoiled this dog, how he had full sofa and bed privileges, how her thirteen-year-old son hardly even liked their own dogs, but had fallen in love with Cormac. I loved the way she called him by name with confidence. There was only a tiny corner of my mind where I would allow this dog in Connecticut to be other than my Cormac.

Then she told me *why* he was getting the royal treatment around her house. "My husband jogs every day along the river," Mrs. Blessing said, "and on the second day Cormac was with us, he went along on the run. Jim fell and broke his ankle. He couldn't get up. Our two Labs just kept right on going, playing, ignoring Jim on the ground. Cormac lay down beside Jim and would not move. Stayed right by his side until help came."

"Wow! I'm proud of him." Then, without missing a beat, I blurted out, "How do I get him home?"

"Now, that I do not know, Mr. Brewer. I expect Mr. Jones will have all that information for you," Erma Blessing offered. "I'm aware the agency uses a pet transport person, and I guess you'll have to pay something, but I don't really know how it works."

"Well, I can't thank you enough for making a home for Cormac," I said. "You folks are probably the first nice thing to happen to him in this strange story. Truly a blessing to me and my dog."

"Why, that's a pun, isn't it?" she asked.

I sighed, suddenly tired. "Yes," I said, "and truly not intended except in deepest gratitude."

TWENTY-FOUR

AFTER TELLING PIERRE and Lou the good news, I tried to phone Drew at his construction site. "Drew didn't answer his cell," I said to Pierre, stepping off the curb. "If he stops by the bookstore, tell him the good news, and to get in touch with me."

"And so you're sure this is Cormac?" asked Pierre. He and Lou followed me to the Jeep.

"I guess until I see him in person, I won't know for sure," I said. "But it all feels right."

"If only we had that collar," Lou said. "You'd know then."

"Well," I said, "I'll know soon enough. I'll phone the agency as soon as I get home, and get things arranged to bring him home." I told them I had to go back on the road Wednesday to finish up the stops on my book tour. "I'll be home Sunday night," I said. "Hopefully, I can arrange to get him down here on Monday or Tuesday."

"Three weeks missing, and you got a lot done in one day," Lou said. "You can rest up some tomorrow."

"I will," I said, thinking I'd really only be able to close my eyes for a good night's sleep when I had him back. I got in the Jeep, rolled down my window and started the engine. "Thanks for hanging in there with me, guys."

"Yeah," said Pierre, "maybe I'll get a dog myself. What do they call them, man's biggest pain in the butt?" Lou clamped his hand around Pierre's neck and slugged him on the arm.

"Go home," Lou said to me, "before you witness cruelty to this animal."

I smiled and waved and eased off, heading for Diana's office. She was on the phone when I got there. I took a seat and looked out the window at the passing cars. I decided to try to keep the news for a minute. When she finished the call, she asked if I'd made any progress today on my rounds, or learned anything about Cormac. I held onto my poker face.

"I got a couple of leads, but they didn't go anywhere," I said. She told me not to get discouraged. We chatted about what I'd do tomorrow to continue the search for Cormac, about her work, about my last few tour stops later in the week. I told Diana I'd pick up the boys at school. I got up to go, stopped and leaned against the doorjamb and tempted her with an offer of pizza at Benny's when she was done.

"You found Cormac," she said, getting up and coming

to stand in front of me. She crossed her arms. "Did you think you could fool me for long?" She smiled and shook her head. "John Luke and Dylan will be jumping when you tell them," she said. "I think pizza is the perfect complement to the news."

"Is that what gave it away?" I asked. "Since that's where we went to mark our decision to get a puppy?"

"No," she said. "We go for pizza like we go for a glass of milk in the morning. It was the goofy look on your face."

"What? I thought I was a man in an iron mask."

"Try silly putty," Diana said. "Don't you know by now that's what Cormac does to you?"

"I suppose so," I said, and I told Diana there was a slim chance the dog I found was not Cormac. "That's when we'll see what I'm made of. Either way, I think, the face is gonna go."

TWENTY-FIVE

I WAS GOING TO SEE a woman about a dog. Her husband, a pet transporter with whom I had made all the arrangements so far, could not complete the delivery of the subject Golden Retriever.

Fenton Jones had recommended this driver, told me the man had made several other dog transports "down South." But the driver would be stopping in Birmingham on other business, so his wife would be making the drop-off, though she could not drive all the way to the coast. He gave me his wife's cell number, and we agreed to touch base as needed to coordinate the exchange in a Cracker Barrel restaurant parking lot at exit 231 on I-65, about thirty-five miles south of Birmingham. She would take only cash. Three hundred dollars.

It was Tuesday, April 5. Cormac had been gone twenty-five days.

Fenton Jones had said he would only release the Golden Retriever into the driver's custody if I would take the dog and agree to keep it, even if the dog was not

Cormac. All the coordinating of schedules had taken about a week, and I'd gone back on the road to New Orleans the previous weekend to make a scheduled appearance at the Tennessee Williams Festival. I had used about half of my allotted time on my panel there telling the story of losing Cormac, and how I'd probably found him and would see him in a few days. People in the audience had been more interested in the dog tale than my novel, and someone suggested I post the rest of the story on my website. Now as the saga's arc would soon put me face-to-face with Cormac, the knot in my belly felt like the alligator sausage I had for breakfast two days ago was trying to bite me back.

It had been almost a month since I had seen Cormac. What kind of shape would he be in? I hoped for happy and hyper, not down and depressed, knowing he'd at least be somewhere off-center on the emotional scale. But, worst of all, what if Cormac were still missing? What if the dog in the van was a total stranger?

The only other time I remember feeling the way I felt as I drove north on I-65 toward Birmingham had been on a certain Friday afternoon some twenty-five years earlier. My stomach, then as now, was queasy, my breathing was in the top of my lungs, my heart was going fast, my tongue was kind of dry. The other time I headed for a rendezvous that had me going like this was when I was headed to see Emily when she was a little girl of two. Emily's mother and I had divorced and I had thought what I needed was to turn off my brain and bend my back in some good old-fashioned heavy labor. That would be the right way to fend off all that mopey stuff that finds its way into country song lyrics. So I called a friend who owned some tugboats and asked him if he'd let me crew. He asked me if I could pack a grip and be ready to ship out the following morning at five. I did, and physically separated myself from the land by working on the deck of a boat rolling on the river. The emotional distance was just the antidote I needed for a wrecked marriage.

Only thing, I stayed on the river too long.

Every day aboard that tugboat got harder and harder, missing Emily. I've still got a photo of me in the tug's galley holding a chocolate layer cake I'd baked on her second birthday. I wrote her name and age on the cake with Cheerios. Missing her birthday did it. I quit working as a deckhand soon as the vessel was docked in the port of Mobile. Hollow echoes of that angst reached me as I drove toward Birmingham.

I rolled past the off-ramps on the interstate, counting upward to my exit. I worried more and more whether it was Cormac I was going to meet. When I would put that fret aside, I'd drag up another one, troubling over what Cormac would do when he saw me. I began to think I should have brought Pierre and Lou with me for some manly emotional support: neither would brook much hand-wringing.

Diana had offered to come. She'd even suggested keeping the boys out of school and bringing them, too. I told her if I knew for a fact it was our Cormac, we'd definitely make this a roadside family homecoming. But since there was at least some chance Cormac was still missing, I didn't think John Luke and Dylan could handle the disappointment if a dog other than our Cormac was on his way from Connecticut. Diana knew that was bull, reminding me we'd told the boys over pizza there was a chance we'd be getting a new dog out of this. She said it was me who'd be a spectacle not fit for family viewing if the dog that hopped out of that van was not Cormac.

Exit 231, one mile the sign said. My heart rate started speeding up. The thumping became so pronounced that I wondered about the physiology of the autonomic response. I considered the advice to take a deep breath. I did. It didn't work, didn't slow down the beating of my heart.

I took the exit, turned right on the service road, and left into the Cracker Barrel parking lot. I stopped the Jeep in the farthest corner, near the grassy median. There was only one way I could do this. I'd have to go inside the restaurant and look out the window. If it was not Cormac in the van, I would need the time, if only a minute, to adjust my attitude toward my new Golden Retriever.

I marched quickly toward the restaurant, refusing to look around, or over my shoulder to see if an unmarked van had arrived bringing my "package." I walked through the store part of the Cracker Barrel to a window at the end of the register counter. I lingered by the T-shirt display, standing there like I belonged with the store fixtures, like a cigar store Indian. Wooden. I think I stopped breathing.

Then I saw the delivery van, a white Chevy. Ironically, it took the parking spot beside my Jeep. The driver stepped out, a woman in jeans and a blue flannel shirt. She rounded the rear of the van and went to the passenger side, where she slid back the door. A dog bounded out. The woman snagged his leash. He had to pee and went straight to the grassy median in front of the van, so that I wasn't able to get a good look at him. I put my hands on top of my head and waited for the dog to walk out so I could have a clear view of him. The woman stood in plain sight, holding a red web leash, the dog at its end still in front of the Chevy. Then she stepped back a couple of paces and she and the dog moved away from the van.

It was Cormac. *Woo hoo*!

And I ran from the restaurant like it was on fire. I didn't look back to see if I'd caused a panic. I just kept running. I yelled *Cormac!* At the top of my lungs I yelled his name again. He spun around on the leash and when he got me in focus, he bolted, snatching the leash from the woman's hand. She took off after him, afraid for his safety in the parking lot, I'm sure. But he got to me and I got to him before she had a chance to intervene. If our lope toward each other could be shown in slo-mo, it would be more beautiful than the way the model ran and tossed her blond hair in that long-ago Breck shampoo commercial: Cormac's red hair flying, my arms out-stretched.

Without even the aid of a leaf, or pair of socks, he found his voice. He whimpered and moaned and twisted his body and flung himself around so that he knocked me down in the parking lot, then jumped onto my chest with me laughing like a fool.

"Cormac, you silly doggins! Don't you ever go away again." He yipped and wiggled and barked and hopped up and down. The woman only stood there watching us as though we were a tree full of hoot owls. I got to a sitting position, and Cormac tried to crawl into my lap like he was an eight-week-old puppy. I remembered the driver.

"I suppose you'd like your money now," I said to the woman.

"My husband's waiting back in Birmingham," she said. "I do need to get going." I stood up and took three new hundred-dollar bills from my pocket and handed them to her. She put the money in her shirt pocket, and extended her hand for me to shake. "He's a mighty fine dog, sir. And mighty glad to see you." She turned, got into her van, and drove out of the parking lot while Cormac and I moved our reunion to the grass median. We rolled and hugged a while longer before heading for home.

After twenty-five miles on I-65, I swung off the highway to grab a sub sandwich at a drive-through. It smelled good and tasted better. When I'd take a bite, I'd give Cormac the next bite. I knew better than to serve the doggins green peppers and lettuce and onions and turkey and cheese on wheat, but we sat there beside each other in the Jeep's two front seats like a pair of college chums headed for spring break, just easing on down South where we belonged, snacking on a sandwich. Until Cormac got sick and threw up.

I stopped at the next exit, pulled into a gas station and cleaned up the mess. As I did so, a man getting into a Buick sedan parked beside my Jeep determined the business I was about. He said I ought to think about riding my pet in a travel kennel, not on the car seat. I told him he should think about riding in a kennel himself. He huffed and slammed his car door and drove away.

Loaded up and driving south on the interstate again, I rubbed Cormac's head and thought again about when I had been so lost in a fog of uncertainty the time I'd spent those six months without seeing my daughter. When I had worked it all out to get Emily for the weekend, you'd have thought I was being granted an audience with the Pope. I went to get a haircut. I bought a new shirt and ironed my jeans. I wondered if a little girl could hold a picture of her daddy in her head for six months.

I was so nervous, my knock on the door that day at Emily's house must have been more like a quiet *tap, tap, tap*. But I can tell you I might have knocked like the landlord, for it went much the way it had just now in the Cracker Barrel parking lot between Cormac and me. Emily had run full tilt across her mother's floor, getting to me as the door still swung on its hinges. She leaped into my arms. She had nestled there and pushed my face away and looked at me and pulled on my ears and patted my cheeks and smiled while I struggled to keep the tears out of my eyes. A weeping prodigal dad would have confused her. I vowed silently to save her from confusion whenever I could.

I looked over at the doggins, Sir Cormac the Mickins, and said, "And to you, best dog in the world, I promise to never lose you again."

I wondered how Cormac felt to be together with me

again. Maybe like this:

I sit on my tail, but it wants to move and I stand as we go and my eyes see the one who has come for me and I lick his hand and it goes onto my head and if he wanted a ball I would get it for him. I will walk close to him. I will lie down to sleep at his feet. We will be together.

TWENTY-SIX

I LIED ABOUT not ever losing Cormac again. Two years later I'd take him for a walk in the woods back of my house, *just this once without a leash*, get distracted studying a twisted root, and look up thirty seconds later to find him nowhere in sight. And spend one miserable Saturday afternoon, evening, and night, calling and driving and walking, my ship being driven farther and farther onto the rocks with each passing hour.

Driving around town, I saw Pierre. "Dogs'll wander, you know," he said. Pierre's nonchalance bothered me.

"And some folks will go looking for them," I said quickly.

I kept checking the front and back doors until one in the morning. I went to bed, but didn't sleep until just before daylight. I was still in bed next morning when John Luke came to find me. He tapped me on the cheek to awaken me. "You were snoring, Dad," he said. "It was loud."

"I'm sorry," I said. "What time is it?"

"I don't know," he said.

"Where's Mommy?" I asked.

"Making pancakes," he said. "Plus, Cormac's outside."

"What?"

I jumped out of bed and ran to the front door in my underwear. I swung open the front door. On the street out front, wet and muddy, grinning, but not about to cross that strange boundary where he would get zapped, was the doggins.

I almost ran out, thought of my pants, dashed back to the bedroom to put them on and ran to the middle of the street. I stood with him, cussing him only a little. I told John Luke and Dylan to get their wagon, and I invited Cormac to jump in and we made it safely to the porch for a good toweling.

"Cormac, I thought we had a deal," I said. I made a plea for him to cease the wandering, once and for all. He grinned. I shook my head. *Your dog thing*, Pierre had said. My dog thing, indeed.

TWENTY-SEVEN

WHEN THE CELL PHONE rang inside my jeans pocket, Cormac cocked his head toward the ringtone as nearly like a bell as I could find from among the device's myriad choices. The interstate was unusually clear and I'd let my speed move past seventy-five, and it was noisy in the Jeep. I slowed to better hear the phone. I guessed it was Diana calling me back. I'd left a message that I had Cormac and we were coming home.

"Hello," I said in singsong.

"Mr. Brewer, this is Tiffany Hale."

"Oh, hello," I said, thinking *now what?*

"Will you be at the bookstore in the morning?" she asked.

"Sure, ah, I can be there," I said.

"I've got the day off and I need to talk to you," she said.

"What time?"

"Ten o'clock?"

"I'll be there," I said. "Can I ask what this is about, Tiffany?"

"I'd rather just talk to you in the morning, if you don't mind."

"I'll see you tomorrow morning," I said.

I ended the call and put the phone in my pocket. "What in God's name now?" I asked aloud. Cormac had his eye on me, as though he knew all that business was about him. "We'll just have to wait and see, won't we?"

I got my phone out again and called Emily at the university to tell her I'd found Cormac. She wanted the whole story, and by the time I'd brought it to the point where he sat beside me in the Jeep, southbound from Birmingham, we were almost home. I also phoned Todd Coverdale, but he was in court, so I left a message with his receptionist.

I ruffled Cormac's ears and rubbed his neck. When my fingers touched the collar, I took note of it for the first time. It was red, and all of a sudden it looked completely out of place, visible remains of his handling and care and keeping by others. "Look, Mr. Mick, I have to tell you you've got a new collar waiting at home," I said, as I unsnapped the red collar and dropped it on the floor of the Jeep. "It's the kind that buzzes you, I'm afraid, and the biggest buzz they sell."

He seemed to listen carefully to all that I told him about how his borders were now more secure than ever. He didn't take his eyes off me, at least. I told him I was sorry, but I knew there would be at least one correction coming his way.

It was the middle of the afternoon when we drove up to our little welcome home party. Diana and John Luke and Dylan were standing in the driveway with Lou and Pierre and Drew. I thought Cormac was going to jump through the open window of the Jeep before Diana got the door open. He bounded out onto the concrete and became such a twisting, turning, moaning blur of red fur that it was hard to distinguish his head from his tail.

The boys sat on the driveway and Cormac knocked them both over trying to crawl into their laps. We were all laughing. All the guys traded high fives with me. Diana gave me a big hug. When Cormac finally took his leave to answer nature's call, I told the story of hiding out inside the restaurant until I knew it was Cormac who'd hopped out of the van.

"It's him, Dad!" Dylan said.

"It's our doggins," John Luke added.

"He sure is," I said. You could not have crow-barred the grin off my face. I saw in my head the missing dog flyer Diana and the boys had made on the computer with the help of our neighbor, Janet, and her Golden, Bailey. Above three pictures of Cormac, they had written MISSING; beneath the photos they'd put REWARD!! CORMAC THE WONDER PUPPY.

I'd not ever told any of them about Rex the Wonder Dog.

But someday I would.

Right now the wonder was named Cormac. With a stick in his mouth, he told me just how good it is when some circles are redrawn unbroken. And the reward was being richly paid out to us all.

TWENTY-EIGHT

IT WAS THAT VERY same day when it happened. Cormac rocked back and forth on his haunches, building his courage to charge the fence line with Dylan and me watching. We sat in chairs on the front porch talking. "Would you look at that?" I said. "Cormac's going to try to cross!"

Before either of us could move, Cormac made a dash forward. The shock hit him hard and it surprised him that it didn't work as it had in the past. He yelped and squealed and barked and ran to our feet, still whining. Then Dylan got angry with me, and asked why didn't I just put up a real fence.

"I'm afraid he'd dig out, son. I don't want to lose him again. Besides," I said to Dylan, "I've got an idea he won't try it again."

John Luke had come around the corner of the house to see what the fuss was about. He patted Cormac on the head and sat down with him on the grass. He, too, took it up with Dylan. "It doesn't hurt that much. It mostly scares him," John Luke said as though he knew this for certain. Dylan challenged John Luke to shock himself with it.

"You're a scaredy cat," Dylan teased.

"Should I, Dad?"

"I don't think that's a good idea, John Luke," I said. But when Dylan taunted him, John Luke insisted. So I told them I'd slapped an electric fence when I was a boy, just to prove to my cousins I could do it. "My grandfather watched from the back porch," I told them. "I walked past three or four cows in the pasture straight to the electric fence. Just walked right up and with my open palm I patted the wire."

"What happened?" the boys asked in unison. I took off my hat and rubbed the bald spot on top of my head, remembering how my grandfather laughed about it for days. "I squealed like a little girl," I said. "It knocked all the hair off the top of my head, and now I have to wear a hat on cold days to keep my head warm." Naturally, they both wanted to know if Cormac was going to have a bald ring around his neck, and I told them that it was a consequence only for humans.

"The main thing is, I never touched the electric fence again. And I don't think Cormac will try to cross his again either."

John Luke decided not to risk going bald then, though

on another day, he'd come in with a pleased look on his face and claimed to have taken a zap from the collar. Dylan confirmed that he had, his eyes big with awe and respect. Dylan wanted to know how quickly his brother's hair would start to fall out. I confessed to my tall tale, but told them to do no further testing with the collar, and that was, indeed, the end of their experimenting.

Also, in all the days from then until now, Cormac has refused to experiment and continues to demonstrate his superior intelligence by keeping well away from the edge of our yard.

TWENTY-NINE

"I'VE BEEN WANTING to call you, sir. But I was nervous. I've got your dog's collar. I wasn't trying to steal it," the young lady said, her words tumbling as if any hesitation would suspend her voice. Tiffany Hale handed me the collar as though she were handing off a snake. Cormac practically stood on his hind legs to sniff it. I gave it to him. He took it and put it down on the floor. He stood over the collar studying it.

"It was just there in the office and your dog was gone and I heard them say it cost two hundred dollars and I thought maybe I could get some money for it and—"

"Wait. Hold on, Tiffany," I tried to settle my thoughts. "So, did it have an ID tag on it?"

"No, sir. But I found it out in the parking lot. That's how I got your number."

"The ID tag was in the parking lot?"

"Yes, sir. That woman who brought him there to the pound, I saw her kind of flick something, but I didn't think anything of it, like maybe it was a cigarette or something."

I said excuse me to Tiffany. "I need to sit down," I said, and walked past the bookstore counter to an over-stuffed and ugly chair near the historical novels section. I was glad Pierre had offered to step outside for this meeting. He said he'd walk to the bank and to the post office. I sat down. Cormac followed and lay down at my feet. I listened closely to what the young woman said.

"Then," Tiffany continued, "when that big man came down here asking about your dog and the collar, I got scared about having it. Also, when he left was when I went looking and found the tag."

"Tiffany. Listen, if you were just then seeing the tag, how did people know Cormac's name?" I didn't want to get into the *Cognac* misnomer at this moment.

"Well, I head that woman say this one will answer to, ah…something. What did you say?"

"Cormac." Cormac raised his head.

"Or something like that," Tiffany said.

"Cognac?" I asked, saying it clearly. Cormac sat up. So, this new name *had* served as a familiar word to him on his adventure.

"Maybe that," she said. "I really don't remember exactly. But something like one of those names, I think."

"Was she handing off the dog to Tara when she called its name?"

"No. Miss Mitchell was at lunch. George took him from the lady."

"Who is George?"

"He's just this guy who works down here sometimes. Not full time. But he's been here longer than Miss Mitchell. At least that's what George says."

"Back to the woman. Have you seen her before at the shelter, bringing other dogs?" An unpleasant image of the woman in the red truck coalesced from the smoke swirling in my head: maybe she had appointed herself some kind of civilian dogcatcher.

"No, sir," Tiffany said. "I've never seen her before. But, I've only been working there about six months. I could ask George."

"If you would, I'd appreciate it. And, too, if she shows up again, would you write down her tag number and call me?"

Tiffany said she would do that, and asked if she was in trouble about the collar. "Will you tell Miss Mitchell?"

"No," I said. "I think she'd give you some trouble if I did." I told her I respected her for having the courage to bring the collar to the bookstore. "That's a mighty big deal, Tiffany. And enough. I don't think anything more needs to be said about it. I really appreciate that you came here in person to give me back the collar."

The girl was relieved. She looked like she thought she

should shake my hand, or something. "I'm really sorry," she said. Only now did she acknowledge Cormac, now that her part in the little drama had completed its arc. She knelt down and called him. "C'mere, boy," she said. Cormac went to her and nuzzled her hand, begging for more petting.

"Please don't think about it any more," I said. "Under the circumstances, all is well, as they say, that ends well."

"Yep," said Tiffany, "I guess he's satisfied with the way it turned out." She tugged on his ear and he rolled his eyes in pleasure.

"I think he is pleased, yes," I said. The girl headed for the door. I followed, with Cormac right behind me. "You sit and stay," I said. I didn't have his leash, and I didn't want him loose on the sidewalk. We stepped outside and I pulled the door closed behind me. I said goodbye to Tiffany and thanked her again. She turned and started up the street. I looked at Cormac, who stuck his nose to the windowpane of the French door. His breath blew little fog images on the glass, and I drifted into a Rorschach thing.

Suddenly, *Ohmigod!* ricocheted down the sidewalk. The voice was high-pitched and it startled me from my brown study. I jerked around and Tiffany Hale pointed toward a red truck passing on the street. "That's her," she yelled.

I looked into the cab of the truck as it drew even with me where I stood on the sidewalk. It was Ruth Baxter! The truck was a seventies' Nissan in pristine condition, shining like a new one. Mrs. Baxter leaned too far forward, both hands gripping the steering wheel. I called her name loudly, but her window was up and she kept going. I wanted to give chase, but Cormac and I had walked to the store that morning. Pierre was still out. I stood there, transfixed by the knowledge that it was Ruth Baxter who had taken Cormac to the pound, that she had removed his tag, that she had lied to me straight in the face. All that about going inside to phone me.

And as it turned out, when I stood at her front door within the hour, her story was simply she did not like my dog. Cormac had been to her house not twice, but half a dozen times.

"I'll tell you young man," she said, "all these dogs running loose. They are just a nuisance. People like you ought to take better precautions to keep the creatures in your own yard." Ruth Baxter actually shook her finger in my face.

"Why didn't you just phone me?" I asked.

"Why don't you have a fence?" she asked.

"I do," I said. "It's an electronic fence. And—"

"Well, it doesn't work. I'm trying to check my mail and here he comes. I holler and he follows closer. So I go to the shed and crank up Ned's truck, which hasn't been run since he died, and I called your dog in the back of it and I took him to the pound."

"Did you know they might've killed him?"

"Did you know a car would've hit him sooner or later? What kind of a way to go is that? At least it's humane how they do it down there."

"And you took off his ID tag?"

"I twisted it right off his collar."

"Mrs. Baxter, I cannot—"

"If you are going to have a dog, Mr. Brewer, you are the one who is supposed to tend to that dog. Not me. As far as I know, you don't even have to go off to a regular job every day. You should have plenty of time to keep your dog at home. If he comes down here again, I'll haul him off again. Now, I'll ask you to leave me alone."

THIRTY

I WAS SHAKY in the knees when I stepped off Ruth Baxter's porch. Cormac sat waiting for me in the Jeep. It's odd to me how he detects my mood and reflects it back to me. He could not have looked a sadder pooch. He would not take his eyes off me.

I looked back toward Ruth Baxter's house and saw the curtain pulled back in the front room, watched it fall back into place. I started the engine and drove in the direction of my house, slowing at the driveway which brought Cormac up on the seat, standing at the ready to jump out and take over his ranch security post. It was just before noon. I thought about calling Diana's office to ask her to join me for lunch, but instead drove past the house, heading for the bay-front park near the municipal pier.

Coming down the hill, the big American flag that flew over the fountain at the center of the rose garden fluttered in a freshening southern breeze. A few cars were parked randomly around the cul-de-sac encircling the fountain. Several people strolled the big pier's quarter-mile extension over the waters of Mobile Bay. I turned right and followed the road into the park area, where a big sign reminded: NO DOGS ON THE BEACH and DOGS IN THE PARK MUST BE ON A LEASH.

"Ah, you dogs," I said to Cormac and sighed deeply. "You're just a lot of trouble. Somebody's got to watch you all the time." I had the windows down on the Jeep, and Cormac nosed the wind, not listening to a word I said. A flock of Canada geese waddled across the road in front of us and I stopped to let them pass. Cormac began freaking out, whining and yelping to get at the big birds. They paid him no attention, heading for the pond in the middle of the park.

"Now see," I said to the Mickins, "if I didn't mind your doings, you'd be raising goose feathers all over the place. And some mean old woman would come and tempt you into her red truck and you'd be gone again." Cormac tried hard to keep his tongue in his mouth. He snapped his muzzle closed, but his eyes were wild for the geese, and his tongue fell out, and then he panted and looked at me as if to say, "Why not? They're just stupid birds."

"Oh Cormac, if you weren't so good looking, so ever-loving cute, I'd trade you for a kayak and paddle aimlessly in the moonlight."

He didn't believe me.

He needed somebody to take care of him.

He knew I was the one.

And that's why he came home.

EPILOGUE

I WATCHED HIM work the room. Being the only dog at a family Christmas gathering gave Cormac a leg up, so to speak, on the territory. In his affable way, he could claim every spot, curl up beside every chair, stretch out on every rug, take all the handed-down turkey scraps, and, more importantly, steal every heart for himself. It was, for the doggins, a gold mine. His dark eyebrows went up and down, flagging his delight.

I had married a good Catholic girl, and Diana's fruitful family had multiplied and there were about sixty people now on hand at the Brewer house to celebrate the season. But the only one of God's four-legged creatures in sight was that big, reddish-brown handsome hunk of a dog. I could see that Cormac would rule this yuletide afternoon, the same way he had taken over our house since his soldier's homecoming. He slept on the bed every night with John Luke. He curled up on the floor with Dylan to watch ESPN.

He still got yelled at for stretching out right in front

of the stove in the kitchen during mealtime, and he was not awarded sofa privileges, at least not often. I watched him move happily from hand to ear-rubbing hand, pat to pat. Somewhere on the floor, Cormac found a toy football and carried it in his mouth, making it easy for him to articulate his approval of these two-leggeds. Cormac smiled and yawned, and I thought he offered all of us a lesson in how to answer the season's hustle-and-bustle: *easy does it*.

Cormac's way was infectious, and I kicked back on the sofa. I was content to let the room buzz all around, without catching much of the buzz myself. And the more I relaxed, the more I fantasized about the hammock strung tight on my back deck. Christmas in coastal Dixie doesn't have very many chestnut roasting days, and the hearth and mantel usually stay cool, lit only by candles, if hopefully festooned with stockings. Cormac ambled over to where I sat and presented his head for stroking.

Then, from the overstuffed chair to my right, Tim, boyfriend of cousin Sarah, asked, "So, Sonny, what's the life expectancy of a Golden?"

There it was.

I did not answer right away because there in that benign query I was confronted with the thought of the end of days for my friend Cormac. Truly, I had never given it more than a passing nod, thinking Cormac would certainly live into his dog eighties or, like myself in my own wishful thinking, into his nineties. That would be, what, twelve or thirteen years?

"Oh I don't know, maybe fourteen years."

"I don't think so," was all Tim said, and crossed his leg. He pulled up his sock and fidgeted with the hem of his jeans. I sat for a few minutes, caught between watching Cormac wander through the people lazing around in the family room and examining this bone that had been dug up, its exposed nub nagging me with melancholic curiosity: what is the life expectancy of Cormac, the Golden Retriever?

Whatever further excavation I might have undertaken was delayed as I watched Cormac, like a playful child, walk straight over and plop down in the lap of Joy, mother of baby Maddie. Joy sat cross-legged on the floor, and the crook of her legs must have put Cormac in the mind of Christmases past when his was a puppy's behind and a good fit for such an inviting Indian pose. It was a comical moment, and Joy's new-mother heart provoked her to do what came naturally: wrap the big lug in her arms. I laughed aloud.

"Toss my digital camera," I called to Diana, standing near the dining room table.

She did just that and my new camera came winging over the heads of cousins Lanny and Graham. I made a good catch, pressed the power button, aimed and snapped a photo of the scene. I'd use the photo as my screensaver image. Cormac left Jay's lap and went to the kitchen to make sure the floor was clear of ham and turkey morsels. I closed the lens cover and slipped from the sofa and went to my study. I spun my black polycarbonate chair around and sat down in front of the computer.

I quickly found a webpage with information about Golden Retrievers. I scanned the topical index until I found *life expectancy*. There was a paragraph of copy that I did not read, because my eye immediately found the phrase, "…about 10-12 years."

The whole screen immediately blurred in front of my eyes.

Cormac in the next room was already six. At the inside, I'd be losing my Mickins before my fifth-grade Dylan entered his sophomore year of high school, and at the outside before Dylan graduated. It did not help matters that one of the two brother Goldens at the top of the webpage looked a lot like Cormac.

And it all really went down hill when Cormac walked into my office. I saw, for the very first time, the whitening of the fur around his muzzle close to his lips. For me, that little thin line of gray there might as well have been a writ from the hand of the Almighty, telling me to bring my dog and a knife and come to the mountain.

"Come here, buddy."

Cormac sat down near my chair, put his muzzle on my thigh and rolled his eyes upward. I thought about a friend who'd gone to a tattoo parlor in New York and had his dog's name, Sadie, written on his thigh just where she'd rested her chin. It had cost him forty dollars. I had forty dollars on me at the moment. But it was Sunday and this was Fairhope. Another time, maybe.

I got out of my chair and sat on the floor beside the doggins. Cormac lay down and turned over on his back and looked at me, rolling his eyes to see better from that position. The whites of his eyes were exposed and it made him look kind of goofy, like he was clowning for a silly picture.

"Mick, damn ye, you're not allowed to die!" His tail thumped the floor, and he seemed to grin at my foolishness. "You're no help," I told him. I got up and went to the hammock on the deck, Cormac trailing me. I took a pillow from John Luke's bedroom, where Cormac sleeps on the bed with him every night now, and a thin lap blanket. At night in the family room, when John Luke is ready for bed, I say to Cormac, "Go with John Luke." Cormac gets up and heads to my son's bedroom, sometimes leading the way. I say to Cormac, "Go find Dylan." Cormac will go find Dylan, and if in his bedroom, then jump onto my boy's bed.

I rolled into the hammock and waited for Cormac to bring his face near. I didn't have to wait for long. "It's not fair, is it, Mick?" Cormac wasn't buying into my funk, seemed more than content to live this one day that was his for the living. He heard a door open, and dashed off to inspect.

I fluffed my pillow and closed my eyes. I just lay there and studied the rope holding me up. I thought about people loving dogs and dogs loving people, which, proved—to me, at least—there was more than science in the universal scheme of things. If dogs just scratched, and people just went to work, maybe I'd doubt God. But with love floating around, senseless love abounding, then I don't doubt divine Providence.

The next day I met Drew for lunch. In the jolly ambience of the noisy café, just a week short of Christmas, around hot and spicy spoonfuls of crawfish bisque, I told Drew I'd just learned Cormac's life expectancy was shorter than I had thought.

"It's like learning Santa Claus is a fake," I said. "The world looks different after you get that little piece of news."

"Didn't you tell me Cormac lost his gonads in his big adventure up to Connecticut?" Drew asked.

"I did."

"If you knew how a male Golden's libido runs him down," Drew said, "you'd know Cormac's got the actuaries on his side for a longer life. Since he came back only *mostly*, missing key baggage," he said, with a locker room wink, "he's also less likely to get smacked by a car while he's chasing girls."

"You're rationalizing this thing, Drew."

"No, I've got this cousin, Smokey Davis, whose dog once left for a week on a romantic romp. The dog got so lost in lust and emaciated he didn't make it all the way back. Smokey found him in the ditch a quarter mile down the road with his tongue out, his coat matted and muddy, nearly dead."

Drew reminded me that Cormac, minus his "wobble sack" stood a better chance of being spared certain cancers and other ailments.

I looked at Drew. "I told my mother I'd present her with a scion of Cormac if anything ever happened to Puggy Bates, her Boston Terrier. Puggy Bates died of liver cancer a month ago, and now I can't make good on my promise."

"You're kind of whining there, pal," Drew said. "You got him back and that's a miracle. You've been put on notice. I got a dollar that says you and Cormac won't miss much with each other. However much time *either* of you has."

"I might even stop yelling at Cormac," I said, "when he shreds the boys' socks. Or, look the other way when he digs a big hole in the yard." I leaned back in my chair.

"I doubt that," Drew said. "Zebbie started chasing my goats again, and he got a good cussing. But I swear he looks like he's laughing when I get mad. And he's got bigger smiles than I've got expletives." Drew drained the rest of his glass of tea.

"You know," I said, "when I was in San Francisco, and got the call from you that Cormac was missing, it occurred to me that while I sashayed around being the writer guy I always wanted to be, I was also busy losing something I love." I told Drew I was one of the lucky ones, getting against big odds another shot to take better care of Cormac. I told Drew about my German Shepherd, Rex, and how he had become paralyzed with hip dysplasia coincidental to the weekend I was away from home. "My father had to put him down in the way country people put down dogs forty-five years ago. It took me a long time to get over being absent when my dog needed me most."

"Well that's bullpucky. Rex is one dog, Cormac is another," Drew said. "You found Cormac because he's important to you. And losing Rex that way does not mean you didn't love the dog. If Zebbie ever flies the coop, I mean seriously gone like Cormac, I can't swear on my mother's head I'd hunt him down the way you did Cormac." Drew added that, compared to what could have happened, this was sort of a fairy-tale ending.

"I was thinking of something a little different," I said, after a moment.

"How so?" Drew asked.

"Do you remember the myth of Parcival and the search for the Holy Grail?" I asked Drew.

"No, but I bet you're about to refresh my memory," Drew said.

"Well," I said, "at King Arthur's Round Table, the Siege Perilous was a chair strictly reserved for only the noblest, most deserving knight. To sit there short of full qualifications meant instant death." I took a sip of tea.

"I remember some of this," Drew said.

"So Parcival sat there, and was obviously the Man for the Chair. He'd just found the Holy Grail. Then, into the hall comes an old hag on a donkey, interrupting the party. She told Parcival while he was out grandstanding his mother died. 'And you didn't even attend her funeral,' she said."

Drew said. "Now I bet you're going to tell me the moral of the story."

"Maybe I'm reaching here," I said, "but all this with Cormac helps me know my life is not just this writing thing. Writing is certainly a privilege and a blessing, but that's only part of it."

Drew pushed his plate away. "No kidding," he said. "Jumping ahead, if you're going to relate the Parcival story to the Cormac story, well, even a carpenter can see the mother in the myth is a symbol for love. So, the knight gave up love for a good seat at the party."

"Right," I said. "And next to a mother's love, I'd hold up a dog's love. A dog left tied to a parking meter has nothing but smiles for the knuckle-dragging cretin who tied him up."

"That's the way of dogs," Drew said. "It's also the way of us men to slay the beasts."

"Right," I agreed. "And while we're out there knifing down dragons, it's a challenge to keep our list in its right order, keep the love stuff at the top."

Drew nodded. "We've also got to milk every moment of all it's got, like it's the last one you'll ever get," he said. "Like this," and for emphasis he tapped the table with his index finger, "this is truly the best day yet. How can it be anything else since it's the only one you've got?"

"Maybe if we can keep all that in mind, we'll still get good seats at the ball. And nobody, and nothing, will be missing."

"Not a soul," Drew said, and winked. "Not a doggone thing."

Acknowledgments

First, thank you David Poindexter for telling me to stop everything I was doing and write the story of Cormac. If your name is among these, then I am deeply indebted to you for the help you gave me with this book: Owen Bailey, Rick Bragg, Diana Brewer, Frank Turner Hollon, Amy Johnson, Skip Jones, Martin Lanaux, Amy Rennert, Shari Smith, Jay Wiley, and J. Wes Yoder. Finally, my gratitude to the incredible people in the MacAdam/Cage offices: Julie Burton, Melissa Little, Melanie Mitchell, Dorothy Carico Smith and Avril Sande. And to Kate Nitze, my editor, and Tom Franklin, my friend, for saving me from myself on every page.

Stephen Savage

Sonny Brewer is the author of the novels *The Poet of Tolstoy Park* and *A Sound Like Thunder*, and editor of the *Blue Moon Café* Southern fiction series. He founded Over the Transom Bookstore in Fairhope, Alabama, where he lives with his family.